# Vexed
# by a Viscount

*An All's Fair in Love Novella*

## By Erin Knightley

Vexed by a Viscount

Copyright © 2015 by Erin Knightley

ISBN-13: 978-1515341833
ISBN-10: 1515341836

# Dedication

*For Kirk, who is happy to share my every adventure with me. You will always be my first choice for everything, even if you do vex me from time to time ;)*

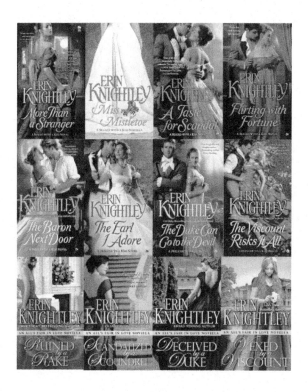

# *Chapter One*

As her toes sank into the slimy muck of the lake bottom, Prudence Landon was beginning to rethink the items on her list. Swimming naked in the lake was supposed to be freeing, exhilarating, and deliciously naughty. Instead, it was cold, dirty, and more than a little disgusting.

Making a face, she paddled backwards, attempting to swim out to deeper water where her feet wouldn't touch the bottom. The farther she swam, the more she imagined some unknown lake creature darting out from its underwater lair and nipping her in the backside. The very thought made her swish her arms around wildly, attempting to discourage any such animal from getting any ideas.

Speaking of ideas, this was a bad one. A *very* bad one. Her only swimming experience in the past had been during her trips to see her aunt in Brighton, where the sea bottom was composed of coarse, firmly packed sand—completely devoid of slime—and the water was clear enough to vaguely see one's toes.

Still, as much as she wanted to abandon her swim and escape to shore, this was her pre-marriage, last-chance-to-live checklist, and by Jove she was going to do it right. The sun was shining, the birds were chirping,

1

the horses were galloping…wait, what?

She froze, nearly going under in the process before remembering to tread water, as she listened over the sudden hammering of her own pulse. That was definitely the sound of hooves pounding the earth in the near distance.

Drat it all! Here she was, naked as the day she was born, her clothes an impossible distance away on shore, trying to do something brave and daring for once in her life and *this* was what happened?

She stayed as low as she could in the water, paddling all four limbs with tiny movements in an effort to keep herself as still as humanly possible without drowning in the murky, creature-filled depths.

A man on horseback appeared through the trees. The horse was moving faster than at a canter, but not quite at a gallop. It was impossible to know his identity—or even his age or hair color—as he streaked through the trees. Her heart thundered away, making it hard to draw a proper breath as she watched him pass within yards of the shore. By some miracle, he didn't turn his head the required angle that would allow him to see her pale pink gown draped neatly over the fallen log by the water.

*Keep going, keep going.* The words ran through her mind like a prayer as she willed him to somehow miss the stark-naked blonde trespassing in her neighbor's most remote lake. Oh heavens, why had she taken the chance? Why had she thought she could break the rules and get away with it?

Yes, she had it on the very best authority that Lord and Lady Malcolm were at a house party a hundred miles from here. And yes, she *knew* they wouldn't be back until just before the wedding, a good fortnight away, but she should have known that the very first time in her life she did anything wrong she would be caught.

Her mother was going to kill her.

No, she wouldn't be that lucky. Mama would simply lock her away until her wedding day, so that she couldn't get into any more trouble on her mother's watch. The very thought made Prudence's throat squeeze. She *needed* these next few weeks of freedom. They were the last she would ever have once she was married off to Squire Jeffries.

Just as she was starting to panic, just when she was sure that she would find herself embroiled in the sort of scandal she had steadfastly avoided for the whole of her twenty years on this planet, the horse and rider passed right by, never slowing in pace nor veering from course.

Relief flooded through her entire body, instantly heating her chilled limbs. Blowing out a quick breath, she started for shore.

And that was when something cold, slimy, and very much alive brushed her backside.

\*\*\*

William, Viscount Ashby, hauled back on the reins, bringing his mount to a jarring stop. *What the devil...?* The horse pranced as he looked around for the source of what he was absolutely certain had been a scream.

A *woman's* scream.

The trees around him blocked any real visibility, so he wheeled around and urged his horse back toward the clearing beside the lake that they had just passed. His blood thrummed through his veins as he scanned the passing scenery. No one should be out here, but he was certain of what he had heard. His father and stepmother were up north for a few more weeks at least, and this time of year none of the servants would venture out to this part of the property, which was reserved for hunting in the fall.

Out of the corner of his eye, he saw a flash of pale fabric against the green grass. When he glanced fully at it, his eyes widened. A woman's dress was laid out as neatly as if it had been draped upon a lady's bed. White unmentionables were folded beside it, and a pair of dainty half-boots completed the ensemble.

With dawning incredulity, he swung his gaze out over the lake, searching for the woman who belonged to the discarded clothes. Much to his disappointment, nothing but wind-rippled water stretched before him. A wry grin tugged his lips despite the letdown. He had come out here for a bit of solitude, but he would have happily made an exception for a nude female.

After glancing around to be sure this wasn't some sort of elaborate trap, he vaulted down from his mount and moved toward the gown. It was no maid's dress, of that he was sure. It was clear, even to a man of his limited fashion sense, that both the cut and fabric were of exceptional quality.

So where had it come from? And why was it here?

Just as he reached out to pick up one of the shoes, a subtle splash and a quick indrawn breath made him jerk upright and swing around to face the water. Much to his astonishment, a flaxen-haired woman rose from the depths, her neck and shoulders bare, her skin glistening enticingly in the afternoon sunlight. He *had* to be dreaming. Or imagining things. Or losing his bloody mind.

But then something clicked into place in his shock-dampened brain, and he realized this was no mirage. He knew this woman, and he would have never, not in a hundred years, imagined her doing such a thing.

"Miss *Landon*?" he said, blinking several times just to be sure.

His eyes did not deceive him. It was indeed shy, timid Miss Landon, the neighbor he had known almost his entire life but to whom he had barely spoken three complete sentences. The same woman who had always been hidden behind acres of ruffled lace and flounces, with necklines up to her chin and bonnets the size of dinner plates shading her pleasant but rather unremarkable features.

Her whole face flamed a deep red as she reluctantly met his gaze. "Lord Ashby," she returned with a dignified nod, clearly trying to maintain her composure.

*Good girl*, Ash thought, more than a little surprised. Any other woman would probably be screaming her head off by then. "Is anything amiss? Should I be worried that bees are about to swarm me, perhaps? Or that a rabid badger is on the loose?"

She sank a little farther into the water. It lapped at her chin as she shook her head. "Not that I'm aware of, my lord."

The evenness of her voice was to be commended, especially when juxtaposed with the abject panic in her vivid blue eyes. Her mother must have spent every minute of the last decade training her to behave like a lady. As soon as the thought entered his mind, he realized the absurdity of it. After all, the girl was trespassing while naked on her neighbor's property.

That thought brought him straight back to the present. More precisely, it brought his attention back to the lovely expanse of pale skin just above the water's surface, in full view of any lucky bastard who just happened to be riding by.

Honestly, he never would have thought sweet, prim Miss Landon had it in her.

"I see," he said, stifling the urge to laugh. "In that case, I suppose I shall leave you to your swim. Do enjoy your day, Miss Landon."

As much as he wanted to stay and find out exactly what she was doing—and perhaps glimpse more than just the tops of her shoulders—his sense of self-preservation was far too keen to allow him to do so. He had been betrothed since he was seven and Tabitha a mere infant, but that didn't mean that someone couldn't find a way to force him into marriage, given a bad enough situation. A situation, for example, like being caught cavorting with a naked young woman of otherwise impeccable character.

She dipped her head. "Thank you, my lord. I'm sure I will."

Lord, but she was a treat. Tipping his hat in farewell, he headed back to his horse, chuckling to himself the whole way. He mounted up, stole one last look, and set off toward the northwestern corner of the property. With any luck, that particular section would be without any unexpected visitors.

More's the pity.

## *Chapter Two*

If it hadn't been for the knowledge that unknown sea creatures were circling her like underwater vultures—at least they were in her now over-active imagination—Prudence might have died of mortification right then and there.

As it was, she scampered onto shore the very moment Lord Ashby and his horse disappeared from sight and sound. Mud squished between her toes as she hurried toward her clothes, all the while dripping wet and covered in goose flesh. Using her chemise for a towel, she hurriedly dried off before yanking her gown on.

This was a disaster. An utter, total, and complete disaster. What if he told someone? What if he laughed about it with his friends at the pub, and the whole village learned of her stupid little rebellion?

Never mind her mother's reaction; her *father* was going to kill her. She'd never done anything to garner his notice, good or bad, but she'd bet her eyeteeth that this would get his attention.

Closing her eyes, she drew in a shaky breath. She needed to talk to the viscount. Immediately—*before* he could talk to anyone else. She sat on the log and brushed at the mud on her toes before cramming her feet in her half-boots. She'd told her mother she was simply going for a long walk to reflect on her upcoming wedding, so she didn't have enough time now to walk all the way to Malcolm Manor, but oh, how she wished she could. Her only option was to go home, then find a way to sneak next door sometime tonight. One more adventure to add to her *Things To Do Before Life As I Know It Is Over* list.

Prudence froze as a fat drop of water plopped on her shoulder. Oh God, her *hair*.

She had purposely requested it be styled high on her head today, with the intention to keep it dry during her little escapade. Now it was a sopping, sodden mess, sagging heavily to one side. It had been a panicked response, diving beneath the surface like that. The possibility of Lord Ashby seeing her had spurred her into action, without a single thought to the fact that she could only hold her breath for thirty seconds or so.

This day was just getting better and better. Fishing the pins from the ruined style, she tried to keep her rising panic at bay. How on earth could she possibly explain wet hair?

She could say she was walking along the stream, slipped, and fell in, but her dry gown would immediately brand her a liar. What other excuse could there be? She wracked her brain as she wrung out her hair and attempted to finger comb the knots out. Being hit in the face with a bucketful of water was downright ludicrous, as was falling head first into a water trough.

As she twisted her tresses into something vaguely resembling a chignon, she tried to think of something— *anything*—that would make sense. She stabbed a few pins into place before dropping her hands to her lap with a defeated groan. Falling into the stream was her most viable excuse. As such, there was only one thing to do.

Gathering her skirts, her remaining hairpins, and what was left of her dignity, she trudged off toward the stream that delineated the Malcolm estate from her own.

In for a penny, in for a pound.

\*\*\*

Nearly an hour later, Prudence got exactly the reception she had anticipated as she plodded through the door, both her gown and her spirits thoroughly dampened. As if by magic, her mother appeared in the front entry hall, her normally pale cheeks overly pink and her eyes wide in abject horror.

Setting both hands over her narrow chest, she said, "Good heavens, child, what happened to you?"

Walking home wearing multiple layers of sopping wet clothing had not put Prudence in the best of moods. Still, the very last thing she needed was to anger or upset her mother. Meeting Mama's widened gaze, she said, "I ventured too close to the stream bank, I'm afraid. If you'll excuse me, I'd like to get out of these clothes as soon as possible."

Mama nodded in earnest, flapping her hand for Prudence to hurry up to her chambers. "Go, go! I won't have you catching your death. I'll ring for your maid and have the kitchen set water to boil for a bath."

Despite the disastrous afternoon, Prudence managed a wan smile. "That sounds nice. Thank you, Mama." Her mother wasn't normally the most solicitous person in the world, so it was gratifying to see her concern.

"Well, we can't have you looking like a half-drowned cat when Squire Jeffries comes for dinner tonight. Now do hurry up. It's going to be a feat to get you presentable in time."

Prudence's already lead stomach clanked to the floor. "The squire is coming to dinner tonight? I had no idea!" No wonder her mother was so attentive all of a sudden.

Dismay flooded through Prudence's veins as she worked out the timing in her head. Blast it all, Jeffries would probably be here until late into the evening. How could she possibly sneak off to Malcolm Manor now? The image of Lord Ashby laughing with friends at the tavern as he regaled them with the story of her nude swim brought heat surging to her cheeks. She *had* to speak to him before the night was over.

Perhaps she could claim illness. After the frigid dowsing in the stream, the possibility of coming down with the plague didn't seem entirely unreasonable.

Mama nodded briskly, causing the graying blond curls that spilled from beneath her mobcap to bob. "Indeed, my dear. He sent word of his intent to visit just after you set out for your walk, and naturally I responded with an invitation to dinner. It's all set, and you can even expect a few moments of privacy with him, now that the betrothal contract has been signed."

This was said with an indulgent smile, as though Prudence had eagerly been awaiting time alone with the man more than twice her age who was soon to be her husband. She drew a deep breath, trying not to linger on the cool buzz of panic that crept up her spine. She was a good daughter, and she would do as her parents instructed, just as she always had.

*The list*, she thought, diverting her anxious mind. It was a lifeline of sorts. Something to look forward to when the rest of her future was too bleak to contemplate.

1. Swim naked in the sunshine
2. Dance barefoot in the moonlight
3. Eat an entire piece of cake
4. Get well and truly foxed

By the time she reached her room, she felt moderately better. These two weeks were hers. For a short moment in time, she would live outside the boundaries of propriety, so that when she was stuck in her gilded prison at the squire's side for the rest of her life—or at least for the rest of *his* life—she would have something on which to look back and smile. Once upon a time, she could say, she had done exactly as she pleased.

Of course, the trick was making sure she didn't get caught again.

Her maid bustled in and quickly divested Prudence of her wet clothes. As she obediently moved this way and that, Prudence's mind wandered back to the viscount—the young, handsome, charming, impossible to talk to viscount whom she'd known almost her whole life, but with whom she had never been able to summon the nerve to have anything other than a perfectly polite, perfectly boring conversation. *I'm well, thank you, my lord. Yes, the weather is just lovely! Do enjoy your day.*

She wrinkled her nose just thinking of what a featherbrain he must think her.

Like it or not, she would have to speak with him tonight. The very thought sent butterflies dancing through her belly. He was just so . . . intimidating. Not in a bad way, but in an out-of-her-reach way. Her family was well-known and respected in their small little corner of England, but it wasn't as though they were part of the beau monde, as Lord Ashby and his family were. She'd never had a London Season, and wouldn't ever be presented at court. She was just a plain country girl who was about to become a plain country wife, destined to live her life shut away in an estate that was miles and miles from anything.

And if that thought made her throat tighten, well then, she could just think of the list.

***

"Mr. Landon has come to call, my lord. Are you at home?"

Ash glanced up sharply at the butler's words. He sincerely hoped his neighbor's presence was a coincidence. After catching his daughter naked—though unfortunately shrouded by murky water—only hours ago, the unexpected visit couldn't help but elicit unease.

"Yes, I'm available. Send him to the drawing room and have some tea sent up. I'll be there presently."

As Tolbert nodded and withdrew, Ash sighed and ran a hand through his hair. God willing, this was merely a casual visit. When he arrived in the drawing room, his neighbor was standing by the window, looking out over the courtyard.

"Good afternoon, Mr. Landon. To what do I owe the pleasure?"

The older man turned and offered a perfunctory smile. Ash breathed a silent sigh of relief. He obviously wasn't here about Miss Landon's escapade.

12

"Lord Ashby," he said with a dignified nod. The long, wispy pieces of hair that had been carefully combed across his thinning pate shifted forward with the movement. "I heard you'd returned, and I wished to be the first to welcome you back."

Right. Having been raised by a father who was legendary for his ruthless pursuit of advantageous connections, Ash could read between the lines. Now that he was done with university, he was no longer seen as the young pup. He was a man now, one with a title, a fortune, and perhaps most important, an earldom in his future. Social climbers were to be expected.

On his guard, Ash allowed his smile to slide toward cool. "Very hospitable of you. I trust all is well with your interests."

"All is well, thank you." Landon paused, cutting his sly gaze toward Ash. "Though I must admit, things would be a lot better if I could convince the earl of the benefits of a joint irrigation project."

*Ah.* Ash had forgotten that his father had dismissively mentioned Landon's pleading on the matter months ago. Shaking his head, he said, "If you can convince the earl to do anything, sir, then you'll have accomplished something quite singular indeed."

The man's lips lifted in a cunning, commiserative grin. "I imagine that as his only son, you must hold some sway with him. I'm a firm believer that this project would be beneficial to both the estates for generations to come."

How little Landon knew of his longtime neighbor. Ash was as much a trophy to his father as his stepmother was. Easy to take out, polish, show off to the neighbors,

13

but never seen as anything of any true worth or value. He couldn't recall a single time his father had asked his opinion about anything, in fact.

Besides, Ash knew his father well enough to be confident he would never agree to the project. The earl wanted superiority over everything and everyone around him. Having superior land to his neighbors was no doubt a point of pride. With complete honesty, he said, "My father takes no one's counsel but his own, sir, I assure you."

Shaking his head, Landon held firm. "You underestimate just how proud he is of the man you have become. Regardless, I hope you'll join us tonight for dinner. A small affair, but certainly preferable to dining alone, I would hope."

It was on the tip of Ash's tongue to decline, but the image of Miss Landon in the lake slipped through his mind. What the devil had she been up to, anyhow? He couldn't help but wonder how she would react to seeing him again. Had she changed so much in the few months since he had seen her? Was it even possible for a mousy little thing like her to suddenly throw off her inhibitions and become some sort of bold temptress?

*Temptress* wasn't the right word. She certainly hadn't been trying to seduce him, of that much he was certain. Still, one didn't simply change one's personality. He was curious about what had motivated her to do such a thing as swim naked in the lake in broad daylight, and the opportunity to learn more had just been handed to him on a silver platter.

Smiling to his guest, he said, "Do you know, I think that sounds like just the thing."

# *Chapter Three*

Without so much as a scratch at the door, Prudence's mother came sailing into her bedchamber, her thin hands fluttering like damp tissue paper in a stiff breeze. "Oh, thank heavens you are presentable. It seems as though we are to have another guest tonight, because of course things like even numbers are of no interest to your father."

Not daring to move her head as her maid jabbed the final pins into her freshly styled hair, Prudence lifted an eyebrow instead. "Oh? Who has he managed to importune today?"

"Viscount Ashby."

Prudence jerked her head around, nearly yanking her coiffure from its moors. Harriet cried out in dismay, but Prudence ignored her. "*Lord Ashby?* Whatever does he want with us?" Her whole body tensed, dreading the answer.

Mama gave a mildly irritated sigh. "Your father went to see him this afternoon, and apparently was inspired to extend the invitation. Normally I'd be delighted to have a lord at my table, but it will make things terribly awkward with the squire here too."

Prudence tried to quiet her growing unease. Mama

had no idea just how awkward things could be. If he breathed even a single word about what he saw today . . . She swallowed. God willing, he had enough sense and discretion to keep his mouth closed. And if he didn't? Well, she would find out soon enough.

A scratch at the door preceded a maid's entrance. "Beggin' yer pardon, ma'am, but Squire Jeffries has arrived. He's waitin' in the drawing room."

"Thank you, Agnes," Mama said before turning back to Prudence. Looking her up and down, she gave a nod of approval. "You look quite well tonight. Your beau will be well pleased."

Mama had been relentless over the years in her attempts to groom Prudence into a proper young lady, but with the coming marriage, she actually seemed to be softening. In fact, her eyes betrayed a hint of pride.

And why shouldn't she be proud? She had produced the most obedient daughter the county had ever seen. Prudence smiled, just as she was expected to do, and came to her feet. There was no use putting off the inevitable. "Shall we?"

Upon their arrival to the drawing room, Squire Jeffries stretched his thin lips into a passable expression of greeting and bowed. He was dressed head to toe in gunmetal gray, with a lifeless white cravat knotted at his neck. "Good evening, Mrs. Landon, Miss Landon. You are both looking quite lovely."

Though his tone held nothing but politeness, his gaze eagerly swept over her form. She had to squelch the desire to cross her arms over her chest. He was her betrothed, after all. However he felt about taking on a wife, it was clear he had no objection to Prudence's figure. In theory, that was a good thing; but in reality, it made her feel decidedly uneasy. Soiled, even.

The problem was that there was absolutely no doubt in her mind that the man wouldn't be marrying her if it wasn't for her tidy dowry and assumed ability to procreate. As her father had stated more times than she could count, a man needed heirs. Squire Jeffries had lived as a bachelor as long as he dared, and was now reluctantly seeing to the task of producing offspring.

And that was where Prudence came in. She knew it was akin to a business transaction, but it didn't get any more personal than having to give over every part of her life and person to this man forevermore.

She bit her lip. There was that dirty feeling again.

Still, regardless of her feelings, he was to be her husband, and she was determined to make the best of it. She lifted her lips in a small, dignified smile and dipped into a well-practiced curtsey. "Good evening to you as well, sir. It is an honor to have you dine with us this evening."

Mama's eyes sparkled with pleasure. Obviously she approved of Prudence's manners. Clapping her hands together, she said, "Oh my, I just remembered that I have to speak with Cook about the final course. Would you excuse me for a moment?"

With all the subtlety of an overeager stage actress, she nudged Prudence toward the squire before scurrying away on her concocted errand.

*Wonderful.* Smiling awkwardly, Prudence gestured toward the sofa. "Shall we sit?"

He shook his head. "No, I think not." Taking a step closer to her, he wet his lips. "With our contracts formalized, I believe a kiss is both expected and appropriate to commemorate our new status."

His pale blue gaze darted down her front before finding its way back to meet her eyes. He looked like nothing so much as a buyer sizing up a potential new horse for his stables.

Swallowing against the disgust that lodged in her throat—he was older than her own father, for heaven's sake!—she gave a tiny nod before raising her right cheek obediently. He was right. A kiss was expected, regardless of whether or not it was desired.

He chuckled, sending his warm, moist breath lapping against her skin. What was so humorous? She may not have ever been kissed, but she'd seen her father kiss her mother at least a dozen times.

Reaching out, he slipped his finger beneath her chin and firmly guided it toward him. With his height and weight remarkably similar to hers, she was left looking directly into his eyes. They were so close, in fact, that she could see the individual spidery red veins extending toward his pupils.

"No, Miss Landon—*Prudence*," he corrected, without even asking her permission. "A proper kiss."

Before she could think of a way to stop him, to invent some perfectly reasonable excuse for him not to press his lips to hers, he leaned forward and did exactly that.

*Oh, good heavens.* She squeezed her eyes shut, but otherwise held still. She was basically already his, was she not? What right had she to refuse him? His mouth was firm and cool. It was almost like kissing a wax figurine. She tried not to think about the fact that this, *her very first kiss*, was with a man more than twice her age.

What had she expected? It was never going to be like the kisses she read about in the scandalous romantic novels her spinster aunt used to hide in her bedchambers. There was no passion, no fluttering heart, no swelling of love within one's breast. Certainly no strong and virile hero fighting to save the woman he loved from certain death.

Aside from the unaccountable relief that his breath smelled pleasantly of lemon drops, she felt only emptiness and dread.

And then it was over. He pulled away after only a handful of seconds and gave a short nod. "I think we shall scrape along well enough. A biddable wife is key to a successful marriage, and with that in mind, I think I have chosen well."

Yes, she was the perfect, obedient young woman she had been raised to be. It was a *good* thing. It meant she had lived up to the standards laid out for her by both her parents and society.

So why did she suddenly want to push him away, escape from the house, and run off to somewhere she could simply be left alone? Such a notion was completely ridiculous.

And this was why she had her list.

She was just nervous about all the changes coming her way. The list kept her mind occupied on silly, inconsequential things. It made her feel as though she were in control of something.

Like her life, perhaps?

She almost laughed aloud at that thought. She never

had been, nor would she be in the foreseeable future, in control of her life. But she could have her private little rebellion. Prudence inwardly cringed. *Not* as private as she wished, actually. Her list may very well come back to haunt her, should Lord Ashby decide to be indiscreet during his visit. Unsettled by the possibility, she quickly stepped back and offered the squire an abbreviated nod.

"I'm glad that you are pleased," she said diplomatically before lifting a hand toward the sofa again. "Why don't you have a seat while I pour you a brandy?"

He smiled, bearing his over-large, yellowed teeth. "Good gel," he said, and she imagined him patting her on the head as though she were a clever child. He sauntered off toward the seating area and she suppressed a sigh of relief. The farther he was from her, the happier she was. Dutifully maintaining a pleasant countenance, she went about the task of selecting and pouring his drink, taking as much time as she possibly could.

Where had her mother disappeared to, anyhow? It felt like ages since Mama had slipped away and firmly closed the door behind her. Prudence would even welcome her father's presence at this point. Unable to delay any longer, she straightened her shoulders and brought the squire his drink.

He accepted the snifter with a nod, then settled back and regarded her as he took a sip. "Have you begun assembling your trousseau?"

She tilted her head, surprised by the inquiry. What an odd question. "Indeed I have. Mama and I spent quite a bit of time with Mrs. Hedgepeth this week."

She would have liked to go to London, or even

Bath, for a more thrilling experience, but Mama saw no reason to go outside of the village when the Hedgepeths had clothed their entire family for nearly twenty years. In fact, Papa was already fretting about where he would find a decent tailor once Mr. Hedgepeth finally put down his needle.

"Bah, the Hedgepeths," Jeffries said dismissively. He glanced to the still-shut door before leaning forward. "There is a modiste in London who knows *exactly* what I like. We'll take a trip there once we are married. The things she specializes in would send Winifred Hedgepeth into a fit of vapors."

What on earth was one to say to such a brazen statement? The thought of him being involved in her clothes and . . . and *unmentionables* made her face flush hot. "I'm sure that won't be necessary," she said quickly. As much as she was dying to see London, this was a trip she would avoid at all costs.

The door opened then, slowly and with a surprising amount of noise, given its well-oiled hinges. Clearing her throat as though she had a lump of dry toast stuck there, Mama made her way into the room.

"Well then," she said briskly, smiling to them both as the squire came to his feet, "everything is settled for dinner. I should mention that Mr. Landon invited Viscount Ashby to join us this evening. He was unaware of our plans at the time, but the viscount is a pleasant enough young man and I'm certain a good time will be had by all."

The squire smiled almost indulgently. "Yes, of course. The boy is probably at sixes and sevens with his parents away. It will be good to see him, as it always is."

Prudence *almost* pointed out the fact that "the boy" was two years her senior, but decided to keep her tongue behind her teeth. It would serve no purpose other than to turn her betrothed's attention back on her.

The sound of approaching footsteps made her glance to the doorway. Her father approached, with Lord Ashby directly behind him. Prudence's belly fluttered unexpectedly at the sight of the viscount dressed in his evening finery. *Good heavens.* The feeling in her stomach was exactly what had so thoroughly eluded her during her kiss with Squire Jeffries. As the two men entered the drawing room, Prudence did her best to train her features into a mask of pleasant indifference.

Nodding to her betrothed, Papa said, "Good evening, Squire Jeffries. So glad that you could join us this evening. You know Lord Ashby, back home now that he's completed university."

"Of course. Known him since he was in leading strings. Not that long ago," he said with a teasing grin, slapping Ashby on the back.

The viscount chuckled, though somewhat stiffly. "Long enough, I assure you, sir."

"I trust your parents are well? I'm looking forward to some grouse hunting when your father returns."

It was jarring, seeing the two men together. Lord Ashby was young, virile, and handsome, with broad shoulders and enough height to look down at them all. In comparison, Squire Jeffries looked like . . . well, whatever the masculine equivalent of *matronly* was. He was thin and short of stature, with salt-and-pepper hair and weathered skin that betrayed his love for the out-of-doors.

Prudence cast her gaze to the floor, chastising herself. Physical appearance mattered not when it came to a man's character. The age difference, however, was a bit harder to overlook. Jeffries had been her age when the French Revolution had begun, for heaven's sake, and that was the sort of event one found in history textbooks alongside the fall of the Roman Empire and Egypt's pyramid-building efforts.

When she looked up, it was directly into the viscount's amused gaze. She promptly straightened her spine, attempting to appear confident even as her cheeks were swamped with heat for the second time in five minutes.

"Miss Landon," he said, dipping his head with exaggerated deference. His lips twitched with humor as he walked toward her. "A pleasure to see you again. It's been *ages*."

"Indeed it has, my lord," she said firmly, widening her eyes just a bit for emphasis. If he spilled her secret now, she would perish from embarrassment. She didn't *think* he was capable of something so cruel, but it was impossible to feel at ease with him standing beside her, his eyes flashing with mischief.

Heavens, but he was handsome up close. She knew that he was well aware of the fact, but his awareness had always manifested itself as playful confidence as opposed to obnoxious conceitedness. He knew he was handsome, but he didn't take himself too seriously.

He pursed his lips as though trying to think. "Let's see, four, maybe five . . . " He paused, drawing out the suspense. ". . . months?"

Her shoulders sagged in relief. He could tease her

all he wanted, so long as he kept the incident to himself. "More like six, I believe. The Christmas party at the Davenports."

"Are you certain? It feels as though it was more recent than that." One eyebrow lifted in playful challenge. It did something to her insides, as though she'd stepped off an unseen ledge. When had he ever teased her before? She couldn't remember a time.

"Quite." She lifted her chin, willing him to let that be the end of it. "Might we offer you a drink, Lord Ashby?"

"Please, call me Ashby, or just Ash. We've known each other long enough to dispense with formalities."

She could almost hear him mentally adding *not to mention the fact I've seen you swim naked.* That would tend to do away with the polite formalities between people. Offering an impersonal smile, she tried again. "A drink, Ashby?"

"Yes, please. Whatever Squire Jeffries is having, thank you."

This time, her father prepared the drink, and another for himself. "Don't know if you've heard the good news, Ashby," he said, returning with two glasses and offering one to the viscount. "The parson's mousetrap has snared Squire Jeffries at last. He and Prudence are to be married in a fortnight."

***

It was the closest Ashby had ever come to spitting out good liquor. *Married?* The squire was a decent enough fellow—odd, but decent—however the man was older than both their fathers. It would be like Ashby marrying someone Aunt Margaret's age. He shuddered

24

at the thought.

Carefully swallowing his sip, he smiled to the happy couple. Or rather, to the ambivalent couple. Miss Landon looked as though she'd swallowed a cricket, and Squire Jeffries merely lifted his glass and took a healthy swig.

"Congratulations to the both of you. May the blessed union bring you great"—he floundered a bit as he tried to think of an appropriate word—"gladness."

*Gladness*? Uninspired word choice, but he couldn't very well say *May the blessed union not bring you misery.* Miss Landon already looked miserable enough, though thankfully no one was focused on her.

It was a telling statement, actually. Here she was, the bride, and neither her groom nor her parents paid her the least bit of attention. So was this what had prompted the little swim today? Was she feeling rebellious, perhaps? God knew Ash wouldn't blame her.

His own betrothal had been arranged so long ago, it was more or less simply a part of him. He had never before considered how lucky he was that Tabitha was so close to his own age. They hadn't spent much time together, but they had plenty in common, and the thought of marrying her in two years when she came out wasn't distressing. It just . . . was.

Squire Jeffries stretched his lips into a pale impression of a smile. "My thanks. Tell me, how are your father's stables looking this year? I know he bought and sold a handful of horses at Tattersall's this Season, and I'm anxious to see the new additions."

Ash allowed the change in conversation, contributing as required while all the while keeping an eye on Miss Landon. She was agreeable, polite, quiet—basically the perfectly bred female. But after discovering her this afternoon, he couldn't help but wonder what lay beneath her placid façade.

What was interesting was that, no matter how she felt about the match, he was absolutely certain that she would go through with the marriage. The next time he saw her, she would be Mrs. Hubert Jeffries. He tried not to curl his lip at the thought. She was disastrously mismatched for the old codger, in his opinion.

It was a damn shame.

# *Chapter Four*

Dinner was proving to be a rather boring affair. Ash really wanted to speak with Miss Landon alone, but with both parents and her betrothed all present, such a thing wasn't going to happen anytime soon. He actually felt a bit of pity for the girl. She kept sending furtive glances his way, a tiny V of worry wrinkling her forehead. Did she really think he would spill her secrets right here at the dinner table?

Yes, he had teased her when he had arrived, but obviously, being a gentleman, he wasn't going to cry rope on her.

As the older men droned on about politics and the state of this year's crops, Ash leaned toward her and offered a reassuring smile. "We are so fortunate to have such fine weather this week, are we not? I'm amazed, actually, that during my entire three hour ride today, I didn't see a single other soul."

Her eyes rounded at his blatant lie, but then she pressed her lips together into a soft smile as her face relaxed. "What a coincidence. I was able to take my walk in complete solitude as well. The sunshine truly was a treat."

That was better. With her forehead smooth once

more, he felt less like a villain. "Are you looking forward to exploring your new home upon your marriage? If I recall correctly, the grounds of the squire's estate are quite impressive."

He wasn't surprised when her features slipped back into the perfectly polite expression he was so accustomed to seeing over the years. "Yes, of course. There is sure to be much to explore."

Now this was the woman he recognized. Well-rehearsed smile, mild tone, neutral response—just this side of vapid, really. But the fact that this persona was back only heightened his interest. What other small rebellions had she been hiding behind that proper veneer? Surely the lake had not been the very first daring act she had ever attempted.

"What other summer activities do you enjoy? Swimming, perhaps?"

Mrs. Landon made a sound of distress from her end of the table. When Ash looked her way, she shook her head and exhaled. "Prudence suffered quite a distressing incident only this afternoon. You must be sure to stay a safe distance from the water's edge in the future, my dear."

Ash's eyebrows lifted. Ah, yes—her wet hair. It should have occurred to him that she would have to produce an excuse for that if she was only supposed to be walking. Thoroughly curious now as to what "distressing incident" she had invented, he leaned back and murmured, "Oh? I do hope you are all right, Miss Landon."

Once again, her fair cheeks took on a rosy hue. "Right as rain, my lord."

The conversation between Jeffries and Landon paused as her father glanced around. "What's this? What incident occurred this afternoon?"

Miss Landon's cheeks darkened incrementally. "It was nothing, Papa. A small slip into the stream."

Ash bit back a grin as he met her sheepish gaze. A slip into a stream, indeed.

"Small slip?" her mother echoed. "You were soaked from head to toe! Thank goodness it is summer. I shudder to think of the state of your health had it been any other season."

The squire's brow lowered as he sent a reproving look toward his betrothed. "You must be more careful in the future, Prudence. A man needs a sensible woman by his side."

Ash took a drink of wine to hide his scowl. How nice of the man to be concerned for his own needs after learning of Miss Landon's misfortune. It may have been a complete fabrication, but Jeffries didn't know that. Showing a bit of concern for her welfare wouldn't kill him.

Ash watched over the rim of his glass as she lowered her eyes and nodded, properly chagrined. Unaccountable anger gathered in his chest. Jeffries had been a friend of Ash's father for years, and he'd always liked him well enough. But seeing him as a bridegroom to the sweet and lovely Miss Landon was putting a rather bad taste in Ash's mouth.

Clearing her throat delicately, Mrs. Landon smiled. "I think it is time to leave the gentlemen to their port. Come, Prudence, let us retire to the drawing room."

As the women came to their feet, Ash and the other

men rose as well. Prudence offered a perfunctory nod before turning toward the door. He wanted nothing so much as to follow her and finally have the conversation he'd been craving half the day, but he was stuck for at least the next ten minutes with the less than inspiring company of the squire and Mr. Landon.

Not the way he had envisioned his evening progressing. By now he'd have been half-foxed and all happy at the village tavern, where he always found himself when he came home. The people there were of the salt-of-the-earth variety, and keeping up appearances was never an issue.

But here? He took his seat and tried not to sigh. Miss Landon wasn't the only one who could grin and bear it.

***

After what seemed like an eternity, but was probably closer to ten minutes, the men rejoined Prudence and her mother in the drawing room. Mama had not been a pleasant companion, fretting as she was about having given Squire Jeffries reason to doubt Prudence's character. That had quickly devolved into her chastising Prudence for having fallen in the stream in the first place, which Prudence couldn't very well defend herself against, since her actual deed had been so much worse.

Had she *actually* fallen in the stream, the reprimand would have been exceedingly unfair.

The very moment the door opened, Prudence popped to her feet, welcoming the others with a smile. Her eyes met with the viscount's first, unaccountably making her heart lurch, but she quickly looked away.

Heaven forbid any of the others suspect her odd
reactions to him.

"There you are," she said, directing her attention to
the squire, as was expected. "I was hoping you'd like to
take a turn about the garden with me. The sunset is
lovely, if nearly over."

He glanced to the oak-trimmed glass doors at the
other side of the room, then shook his head. "I think not.
The air inside is much more pleasing to me, as is the
prospect of another drink."

*Drat*. Smiling through her disappointment—she
really did wish to be free of Mama for a moment, even if
it meant spending more time with her betrothed—she
nodded and made to retake her seat.

"It does look like a rather extraordinary sunset,"
Ashby said, his head tilted as he looked through the
windows. Turning his attention to Prudence, he lifted his
eyebrows. "If you don't mind somewhat inferior
company, and if your betrothed wouldn't mind if I
provide escort, I would very much enjoy a little time in
the garden."

"Perfect," she exclaimed, a little too quickly.
Tempering her voice, she added, "The weather is ideal
for a stroll, I think." There—a banal comment about the
weather. No one should suspect just how badly she
wanted to speak with him alone.

Politely looking to the squire, Ashby waited for his
approval. When the older man nodded with a dismissive
wave of his hand, already heading toward the sideboard,
the viscount grinned. "Very good. Shall we, Miss
Landon?"

She tried to ignore the very improper flutter in her

belly as she nodded and accepted his proffered arm. "Lead the way."

He smelled of wind, grass, and the lingering scent of cheroot smoke. She hadn't realized until that moment how much she liked the smell of grass. Had she ever been on his arm before? Felt the firm outline of his forearm? Beneath the layers of lawn, leather, and wool, of course.

She firmly pushed away the silly romanticism of his arm and concentrated on walking like a normal person as they made their way through the doors, past the small terrace, and into the rose garden beyond. The sky was a vibrant pink, providing a perfect backdrop for the blooms.

"At last," Ashby said, sending her a rather mischievous glance. Up close like this, she could see his brown eyes had a mossy green rim around his pupils. Tiny flecks of yellow spangled the line between the two colors. "Please, for the love of God, explain to me what I witnessed today. I can't take the suspense a moment longer."

He wasn't one to beat around the bush, apparently. It was quite possibly the most direct thing anyone had ever said to her. Momentarily flustered, she shook her head and concentrated on the nearest rosebush. "It was nothing. A silly, stupid whim that shan't be repeated, I assure you."

"Well, that is a disappointment."

Prudence glanced up sharply, incredulous that he would say such a thing, but the moment she met his gaze she could see that he was baiting her. It wasn't something she was used to. How exactly was one supposed to respond to a handsome gentleman teasing one in the garden?

Straightening her shoulders a bit, she said, "Nevertheless, it is the truth."

The viscount stopped walking, and pulled his arm away so he could face her fully. The evening light gave his skin a rosy glow and made his eyes shimmer. "Fair enough. The question remains, however: Why would a perfectly proper, perfectly *betrothed* young woman step so thoroughly off the straight and narrow path?"

It was hard to think when he was so close, watching her so intently. Despite the levity in his eyes, she knew he intended to root out the truth. She glanced down and fussed with her gloves, buying a moment to gather her thoughts. "As I said, a whim."

"One tries a new hairstyle on a whim. One decides to visit a good friend on a whim. One does not swim naked on one's neighbor's property on a whim. *Especially* when one's name is *Prudence*." His hands went to his hips as he lifted an eyebrow and waited for her response.

She blanched a bit at his frank words. Glancing around to be absolutely certain no one could have overheard, she said, "Please, do not speak of it. I have admitted to how ill-advised it was, and I am attempting to pretend it never happened."

"I see. In that case, let us talk in hypotheticals. A young woman of impeccable manners and with an exceptionally well-regarded family decides to do something utterly outrageous. Why, I wonder, might she suddenly decide to do such a thing?"

Hypotheticals. Yes, she could do that. Lifting her

shoulders in an *I'm-merely-speculating* sort of way, she said, "Perhaps one doesn't want to live one's entire life without some small adventure."

Nodding thoughtfully, he turned and began to walk again. She fell into step beside him, hoping against hope that he would drop it.

"An adventure. But if one is young, there will be ample time for adventure. And entire lifetime, really."

"Unless one is about to be married off to someone decades her senior who prefers to sit indoors on a perfectly lovely evening and bypass such things as dinner parties and dances whenever possible. One could shortly become stuck in one's new life, particularly when one has children."

He cut a glance her way before setting his gaze on the flagstone path before them. "Hmm. Yes, I see how one would feel the need for adventure. *I* feel the need for adventure, just hearing of such a fate."

A small seed of panic bloomed in her belly as she realized how very honest she had just been. What was wrong with her? Was she so desperate to let out her worries that she would speak so frankly to a man who was little more than an acquaintance?

Yes, actually.

Desperate was exactly what she had been feeling lately. Was that not what had caused her to act so rashly in the first place? "And there is no harm in it. Assuming one is discreet . . . as is any person who may accidentally stumble upon the adventure."

He nodded, only the barest hint of a smile gracing his lips. "Yes, I imagine that is key."

They had already wordlessly established as much at

dinner, but it did make her feel somewhat better to have it said aloud.

"I wonder, though . . ."

She waited, but he didn't say any more. Against her better judgment, she couldn't help but give in. "Yes?"

"What other adventures does one have planned?"

She gaped at him. How did he know she had a list?

His teeth flashed white as he smiled hugely. "Aha—so you do have more adventures planned."

"Of course not!" she exclaimed, even as the full heat of a blush assailed her whole face. The hypothetical had given way to her reality entirely too quickly for her peace of mind.

"Come now, you needn't worry I'll divulge your secrets. I've proven my trustworthiness thus far, have I not?" He gave her a coaxing, overly-familiar grin as he leaned forward an inch or two. "Now then, am I to find you streaking bareback through the countryside? Commandeering a hot air balloon? Joining a band of highwaymen, perhaps?"

Try as she might, she couldn't seem to stop herself from smiling at his outrageous suggestions. "You must think me daft. I have no intention of attempting anything so daring or illegal."

"Then what do you intend to attempt?"

"A few small rebellions. Nothing anyone other than my mother would find outrageous."

"Such as . . . ?"

She plucked a leaf from the rose bush beside them, wishing she would have stayed inside and avoided this embarrassing conversation. "Dancing."

"Dancing? Surely you've done so before."

"Of course I have."

"Then how is this a rebellion?"

"Dancing barefoot in the moonlight is not exactly an accepted convention."

He lifted an eyebrow. "My, but you reach for the stars when coming up with your adventures."

She may not be one to make use of sarcasm, but she certainly knew it when she heard it. "It needn't be unwise or dangerous—merely *freeing*."

"I see," he said, actually appearing to take her answer seriously this time. "And when is this dance to occur?"

"The full moon is two days away, so it seemed a rather appropriate time to do such a thing."

"I agree completely. What else is on the list?"

Taking a deep breath, she decided to simply tell him and be done with it. She was obviously unable to keep any secrets from him. "Eat an entire piece of cake, and get thoroughly foxed."

Both eyebrows rose at this. "At the same time? I can't say I recommend it."

"No, not at the same time. I figured I would save the spirits for the eve of the wedding, when I'll likely need it most."

Shaking his head, he gave her a small smile that somehow straddled the line between pity and amusement. "Yes, I imagine you will. Also, I never thought dessert would be on an adventure list. What's wrong with simply eating a piece of cake?"

Mimicking her mother's legendary lecturing tone, she said, "A lady never devours her dessert. A healthy appetite is unseemly for a woman of good breeding. A bite or two if you must, but always set the fork down with your plate mostly untouched."

He looked aghast. "But dessert is the very best part of life. How do you bear it?"

"Restraint is a virtue," she replied, before blowing out a small unladylike sigh and smiling wryly. "I cannot abide any sort of conflict in my life. It's always been easier to do as my parents asked, and to behave as expected. It's not as though I have any grand plans outside of those expectations, at any rate."

"Save for eating cake, of course."

She smiled. "Yes, there is that."

He straightened abruptly, leveling the full force of his handsome brown eyes directly on her. It was rather dazing. "You, Miss Landon, shall eat cake. Will you meet me tomorrow at the property line?"

Her mouth fell open just a bit before she had the wherewithal to pull herself together. "You wish to see me eat cake?"

"I wish to eat cake *with* you. And I wish to provide it. What time works for you?"

She bit her lip, trying to hold back the little thrill of excitement that raced through her at the look in his eye. He was not only serious, he actually looked somewhat indignant on her behalf. No one had ever been indignant on her behalf. The only champion she'd ever had was herself, and she was doing a terrible job of it.

"You really needn't—"

"Eat cake?" he interrupted, a devilish grin tilting the corners of his lips. "Yes, I need to. One should always eat cake. And if you won't meet me, then I will be forced to share with the birds because no matter what,

I shall be at the path between our properties at three tomorrow afternoon, cake in hand, so you might as well join me."

*Good heavens.* She looked up into his eyes, astonished and thrilled and more than a little giddy that he should actually care about her and her list. "Very well, then. I shall see you at three."

"Excellent," he said, thrusting out his arm once more. "Now I suppose we should get back to the party." There was no mistaking the sarcasm the word held. Obviously the evening hadn't been his idea of entertainment.

Without a word, she slipped her hand over his sleeve and allowed him to guide them back toward the house. All the while, she reveled in the feeling of being *seen*. Paid attention to. Perhaps even cared about.

Another thing she could add to her list of adventures: Be thrilled by a viscount.

# *Chapter Five*

Ashby didn't know why he should be so bothered by Miss Landon's situation, but he was. Truly—whose life goal was to eat an entire piece of cake, for God's sake? He wondered if the girl had ever had a day in her life when she could simply relax and enjoy life

Combined with the fact that she would soon be yoked to the squire—who was as well matched to her as a fish would be to a cat—Ash wanted nothing more than to give the poor girl her little adventures.

After all, he was well versed in the art of enjoying oneself. He was lucky to have inherited—by all accounts, since he himself couldn't remember—his mother's lighthearted manner. He had no need for the power-grasping lifestyle of those like his father, nor the more staid, rule-abiding existence of people like the Landons.

What was the point of life if not for a little enjoyment?

With his betrothed still in the schoolroom and his responsibilities far in the future, he savored every minute of his life these days. Live for the present, *carpe diem*, et cetera. Clearly he was the perfect candidate to help Miss Landon.

He arrived at the door just as the butler swung it open. As he divested himself of his hat and coat, he said, "Evening, Tolbert. Fetch Cook for me, would you?"

The older man didn't show a hint of emotion. "As you wish, my lord. It might take a moment, as she has retired for the evening."

Yes, of course she had. Ash hadn't considered the fact that it was after ten and the kitchen staff generally rose before the sun. "No, don't bother her. But do convey to her that I would like an assortment of cakes for tomorrow afternoon. Two or three should suffice."

Tolbert nodded. "It will be done, my lord. Is there anything else you require this evening?"

"For you to retire as well," Ash said with a grin. "Thank you for your excellent service as always, and I bid you good night."

The tiny lift to the butler's eyebrow was akin to an eye roll from anyone else. None of the servants saw him as anything more than the young, mischievous boy he had once been. Not that Ash really blamed them.

Aside from the fact they had known him since he was an infant, he was in the exceedingly unusual situation of having an older brother, yet being the heir. Nicolas was technically Ash's stepbrother, but he had come into the family when Ash was only five, so he really didn't have any memories of a time when he hadn't looked up to his older brother. As a result, no one save the earl had ever really looked to Ash as a future authority figure. Even Ash had a hard time picturing himself as lord of the manor someday.

Just as he had a hard time picturing himself as a husband someday. He wasn't opposed to the match—

Tabitha was a sweet, lovely girl, to be sure—but she was still too young to imagine her as his wife just yet. When she turned eighteen in two years, he was hoping the age gap wouldn't seem so wide. Maybe then she would seem less like a younger sister or cousin and more like a partner.

It was a rather large *maybe*.

But he was lucky. At least he wasn't facing a thirty-year age gap like poor Miss Landon. Sighing, he scraped his hand through his hair. She would have her cake, and she would have her dance, and she would get drunk as a broken wheelbarrow, by God. The rest of her life was up to her, but for the next two weeks, he fully intended to help her live.

***

What, exactly, was one supposed to wear to a clandestine meeting with a viscount that was to prominently feature the eating of pastries? As Prudence strolled down the winding path toward the woods, she contemplated her rather cheery yellow frock, with its perfect little cap sleeves and frilly white trim. Was it too sunny? Did she look as though she were trying to impress him?

Because she wasn't.

Very well, so that was a lie. For some indefinable reason, she'd wanted to look nice today. If he were a bit less handsome, she doubted she would have worried so much about her choice of dress. She sighed. That was another lie. Yes, he was handsome, but his attractiveness to her had always been more than that. He was easy in his own skin, confident without being cocky, and always quick with a smile. He never seemed to have a problem with speaking his mind, but more to the point, he managed to do so without rocking any boats. It was a trait she had admired for years.

Their conversation last night in the garden had been the longest they had ever engaged in. Instead of tempering her positive view of him, it seemed to amplify it. She shook her head as she stepped over a small fallen branch. All of this was quite ridiculous. This whole thing was supposed to be about her list, not the man who had managed to ferret out her intentions and offered himself up as helper.

Cake. She was meeting him to partake in cake, and then she could cross another item off her list. It was as simple as that.

As she approached the clearing where their properties met, she caught sight of him lounging on a wide blanket, a huge wicker basket at his elbow. It was an idyllic, bucolic scene, straight from a landscape painting. Sheep on the far hill, tall grasses all around them, bright blue sky with the occasional puffy white cloud above them . . . All it needed was a mare and foal grazing in the distance and the moment would be pastoral perfection.

Rising to his feet, he dusted off his breeches before waving to her. "Good day, Miss Landon. I was beginning to wonder if I would be eating alone this afternoon."

She gave him an apologetic smile. "I'm sorry to keep you waiting. I was unavoidably detained." Waffling on which gown to wear—a fact she had no intention of sharing.

"Well, you are here now," he said with a dismissive

flick of his hand. "You'll be happy to know that I miraculously managed *not* to eat any cake yet."

"Your willpower is to be commended," she replied, sharing a grin with him.

"And it is at the end of its rope. Come sit so we may partake. Delaying gratification has never been one of my strong suits."

He held out his hand and she readily accepted his assistance. His touch was polite and impersonal, perfectly correct in every way, but still she felt it all the way to her belly. Had she ever met with a man alone like this before? The answer sprang to mind before the question had even fully formed: of course not. Her mother had diligently protected her from any situation that might be construed as unseemly.

As he settled down beside her on the blanket, he flicked open the basket lid and retrieved a small but glorious iced cake. "I hope you like lemon," he said as he presented it with a flourish.

Her mouth watered at the very sight of the thing. She nodded, smiling. "I love lemon, thank you."

He set it down, then reached inside the basket again. Looking rather pleased with himself, he extracted a pink-hued cake in one hand, and another iced dessert in the other. "But there is also raspberry, if you prefer. And plum cake, because that's my personal favorite."

Prudence shook her head, unable to believe that he had gone to such trouble. She was practically nothing to him. That he would go so out of his way when those who were much closer to her wouldn't even think of it was as disconcerting as it was wonderful. "You really, really shouldn't have, my lord. What on earth are the

43

two of us going to do with three whole cakes?"

Even as she protested, her gaze drifted back to the delectable treats before them. She couldn't wait to finally enjoy as much as she wanted, without her mother watching and counting every bite she took. A silly indulgence, to be sure, but one that she would relish with every fiber of her being.

"Devour them, of course," he said, recapturing her attention. His greenish-brown eyes glinted merrily in the afternoon sun as he produced two plates, two forks, a knife, and several napkins. "And do call me Ash. I don't wish to stand on ceremony while lounging at a picnic."

"As you wish. Would you like me to serve?" She well knew how to be a proper hostess, but this little interlude was outside of her normal experiences.

He shook his head. "I shall do the honors. This is your moment. I am merely here to facilitate."

They had only been together for a handful of minutes, but already this was one of the best afternoons in recent memory. Not wishing to rush the experience, Prudence pursed her lips and gave the suggestion due consideration, carefully considering each of the cakes. "In that case, I believe I shall have a slice of the lemon, if you please."

"You will do no such thing," he said, his left eyebrow lifted imperiously. "Today you are to indulge, in every sense of the word."

She watched, eyes wide, as he cut thick slices from each cake and piled them onto her plate. Laughing when he presented it to her with a flourish, she said, "I couldn't possibly! You'd be carrying me home, were I to eat all this."

Ash sent her a devilish grin as he quickly filled his own plate. "I'm wholly up to the task. Now," he said, lifting his fork in a sort of salute, "let us eat cake."

Barely able to contain her rising giddiness, she bit her lip and returned the salute. She filled her fork with a heaping morsel of lemon cake, added a bit of raspberry cream, then put the entire unladylike-sized bite in her mouth. The explosion of sweet, tart, lemony deliciousness was good enough to make her moan, and she closed her eyes to fully savor it.

This was heaven. Better than heaven—this was forbidden fruit. Nothing ever tasted so sweet as that which one wasn't supposed to have.

"Where was this person all these years?"

Her eyes popped open to see him watching her, obviously amused. Suddenly embarrassed for having so thoroughly abandoned propriety, she straightened her shoulders. "I'm not so very changed. At least, not on the inside." For all the times she would have never acted on her sometimes imprudent thoughts, she had still had them.

"Well, I do wish I would have known this person a little better. We might have had more fun together growing up. Once Nicolas left for the army, things became rather boring during my visits home."

She took another huge bite of cake—this time the plum—while she contemplated his comment. It was no secret that his father was a terribly unpleasant man. Her own father heartily disliked the earl, even as he tried to sway him to work on the irrigation project together. Still, Ash had always seemed so thoroughly happy with life. Had he been lonely?

"And here I imagined you led quite the charmed life."

"Oh, I do," he said, chuckling when her eyes widened at his honesty. "With all the privilege heaped upon me, I'm not very well going to disparage my good fortune. But even so, it's easy to feel isolated in an area where one's family is held in such high esteem."

*Isolated* was exactly the word she would use to describe her own upbringing. "That I understand. My mother was very keen to keep me from those of inferior social rank. As though one's status was catching."

He gave a little snort. "If we felt that way, I'm not sure if we'd ever have talked to anyone when we were in residence. Of course, that doesn't mean that my father doesn't do everything in his power to align himself with those of higher ranking."

She gave him a wry smile, her next bite poised before her lips. "I know the feeling," she said before popping the cake in her mouth.

Setting down his fork, he tilted his head and looked at her. "Which makes me wonder why we weren't in each other's company more growing up."

That was an easy one. "You were betrothed," she said plainly. "Mama didn't see the point."

He barked with laughter. "Well, that's honesty for you." Recapturing his fork, he went about filling it. "As much as I might have preferred to pick my own spouse, I must admit that a lifelong betrothal makes for fantastic match-making-mama repellent." The cake disappeared into his mouth. As he chewed, the corners of his lips remained lifted with mirth.

His words actually surprised her. "You would have

liked to choose your own wife?" He was a man; she'd assumed he would have already protested the arrangement, if that were the case.

He shrugged as he swallowed. "Of course. Who doesn't want to have a say in who will sit across the breakfast table for the rest of one's life?" As if realizing the implication, he grimaced and said, "My apologies. I realize that you are in a situation that is certainly outside of your control."

*Control.* What a foreign concept for her. "Nothing in my life has ever been in my control, so I have no reason to protest now." She stuffed another bite of the lemon cake in her mouth. It really was divine. Light, fluffy, sweet, and tangy. It almost made up for the distasteful turn of the conversation.

He shifted, leaning on his left arm while lightly tapping the prongs of his fork on the plate. Regarding her thoughtfully, he said, "Have you never before rebelled? Tested the waters of disobedience?"

The very thought made something inside of her cringe. "Perhaps when I was very young, but honestly I can't remember ever doing so. My parents' and nursemaids' wills were law to me. There's this heavy lump of dread that lodges in my chest if ever I think of pushing back. I swear I am physically incapable of being defiant."

Even now, sitting here in the sunshine eating the world's most delicious cake beside one of the most charming men she knew, there was still an echo of that lump. The only reason she had been able to pursue the items on her list was because she was doing so secretly. Or at least as secretly as one can be with an accomplice.

"And yet, you have a list."

She nodded. "I do." Drastic times called for mildly drastic measures.

"And you are actually doing the things on the list." He sounded as though he were genuinely impressed.

A small, pleased smile tugged at her lips. For the first time in her life, she was stepping outside of the straight and narrow path she had held to for so long. "I am."

He lifted a heaping forkful of cake as though it were a glass of champagne. "To Miss Landon. The bravest woman I know."

There was no holding back her grin now. "Call me Prudence." Even just saying the words sent a rush of exhilaration through her. Right then and there, she decided that *Extend the right to use my Christian name to a handsome man* should definitely be on her list.

His answering smile sent a second rush clear to her toes. "Actually, I believe I shall call you Pru."

*Pru?* She wrinkled her nose. "Whyever would you call me that?"

It was impossible to miss the devilish glint in his eyes. "Because for the next two weeks, I declare that you shall be as *im*prudent as possible."

The confidence that rang in his voice made her feel that much more daring. He believed she was capable of breaking from her prison of correct behavior. Of course, he *had* seen her swimming naked, so perhaps it wasn't such a great leap for him.

His grin turned teasing as he leaned forward. "And you may call me William if you wish to be truly naughty."

"Oh, I can't imagine . . ." She bit her lip, contemplating whether she could bring herself to call him that. "Are you certain?"

He lifted his shoulders in a small shrug. "Quite. Though really only my brother and cousins call me that. My father has called me Ashby since I was born, as do all of my school friends, and that's more or less how I think of myself."

*William.* She silently mouthed the name, feeling terribly forward all the while. Finally, she shook her head. "Ash will suffice, I think. Since that's what you call yourself."

It was obvious he wasn't fooled. Lifting an eyebrow, he said, "Mm-hmm. Very well, but I must insist that you say it, at least once."

"No, really—"

He cut her off. "No arguments. Say my name."

For some reason, the request sent a tiny thrill straight down her spine, making her shiver. It was just so . . . *personal.* "It's not necessary—"

He set his hands on either side of her shoulders, immediately stealing the air from the rest of her protest. "You're thinking about this too much. Let go of convention, throw that exceptionally well-developed caution of yours to the wind, and call me by my Christian name."

For a moment, she couldn't speak at all. She was held spellbound by his earnest gaze and the warmth of his hands at her shoulders. The flecks of gold in his eyes seemed to shimmer like sunlight dancing along the forest floor. Taking a long, slow breath, she licked her lips and met his gaze. "As you wish . . . William."

# *Chapter Six*

Ash's breath rushed from his lungs like air from a bellow. No one had ever spoken his name quite like *that* before.

In the space of that one word, the lightheartedness of the moment evaporated like water in a hot pan, leaving him momentarily stunned. What the hell had just happened? He leaned back, breaking the contact between them, and rubbed his hand over his chest.

Those big, sapphire-blue eyes stared back at him expectantly, uncertainty lurking in their depths. He rallied, knowing he needed to respond. "There, see? That wasn't so hard, was it?"

His voice sounded normal, thank God, and he could almost pretend the strange moment hadn't happened. He was doing nothing more than helping a neighbor. Wasn't that what people were supposed to do? It was even in the Bible, if he wasn't mistaken. Or maybe it was love thy neighbor . . .

Shaking himself from the strangeness of his reaction, he settled back and grabbed his fork like a lifeline, shoveling another chunk of the plum cake into his mouth.

She made a face, or at least as close to a face as one

as ladylike as she could make. "Yes, it was hard, actually," she said, her plump bottom lip falling victim once more to her top teeth. Still, there was a hint of teasing in both her words and her eyes. "But at least I can scratch it off my list now."

Feeling on firmer footing again, he chuckled. "Am I on the list now? I recall only swimming, dancing, eating, and drinking."

"I'm not opposed to revising the list," she said, primly brushing crumbs from her skirts. "*Address a social superior by his given name* was added mere moments before it was accomplished."

"So we can add to the list?" He liked that. If she was about to resign herself to a life with Jeffries, he wanted her to enjoy the next few weeks as much as possible. His mind flipped through a dozen possible scenarios to add to the list. "This just got much more interesting."

She shook her head, pressing both hands to her chest. "*I* can add to the list. I'm not certain it would be wise to allow *you* to do so. I can just imagine all manner of troubles you would get me into."

"Yes, I can too," he agreed, earning a light laugh from her. "Perhaps there is a compromise in there. Allow me to add just *one* item to the list. One that I promise will not land you in front of the magistrate or warrant your parents' censure."

Eyeing him suspiciously, she said, "And what, exactly, do you have in mind?"

"I don't know yet. But I brought you cake, so that should count for something."

"It does—my heartfelt gratitude. It does not entitle

you to my blind trust."

He liked bantering with her like this. She'd lost any hesitancy that she had shown in the past, appearing to be truly at ease with him. Which was appropriate, seeing how that was precisely how he felt with her. "Then I shall have to prove my trustworthiness," he replied.

She pulled her bottom lip between her teeth again, briefly worrying it. "I see. And how do you plan to do that? I wish to know if I should be worried or not."

He smiled broadly, if purposely enigmatically. "There's time enough to worry about that. But for now," he said, confiscating her fork in order to lift a morsel of lemon cake to her reddened lips, "you still need to finish your cake."

Surprise registered in her gaze, but just when he thought she would refuse him, she opened her mouth and accepted the bite. He loved watching her savor it, as though it were the finest dessert ever to pass her lips. She showed more pleasure in this small thing than some of the women he knew showed in gifts of jewels.

When she finished, she looked down at the still half-full plate and sighed. "This was amazing, but I can't possibly eat even one more crumb."

"I think it counts for crossing off the item from your list. After all, if you partook in half of three small slices, that equals one regular slice."

Her laugh was as light as goose down. "Yes, I do believe you are right."

"And was it everything you hoped it would be?"

Her smile softened as she nodded, her eyes never leaving his. "Much more so. Thank you, Ash. You turned quite an ordinary event into something rather extraordinary."

In that moment, he wanted to go to Jeffries and demand that he give his bride cake every night. Anyone who appreciated the small pleasures in life this well deserved to indulge.

Nodding, he said, "You are most welcome. I don't think I have enjoyed cake or company quite so well in my life."

"My feelings exactly. Alas, I must return home. My mother will begin to worry that I fell in the creek again," she said with a wink.

"Those creeks do tend to sneak up on a person," he said with a grin. "Can I at least walk you back to the edge of the forest?" The idea of having her leave so soon was more disappointing than he would have imagined. He stood and held out his hand to her.

She readily accepted his assistance, slipping her gloved hand into his and allowing him to lift her to her feet. "No, I think not. I would hate to try to explain your presence should someone come upon us."

It was sound reasoning, unfortunately. "Very well. Thank you for joining me this afternoon. I do so love abetting a bit of debauchery." He gave a teasing wiggle of his eyebrows, wanting to see her laugh one more time.

He was not disappointed. She wrinkled her nose and half laughed, half groaned. "I am involved in no such thing! Debauchery, indeed."

"Well, what would *you* call the willful abandonment of propriety?" he challenged, sending her his most innocent look.

Swatting at his arm, she said, "Merely sidestepping the rules for a moment or two." She lifted her chin, practically daring him to contradict her.

Sweeping his most magnificent bow, he said, "Then who am I to disagree?" Straightening, he smiled with genuine affection this time. "Good day to you, my friend. I do look forward to seeing you again soon."

After a brief curtsey and cheeky grin, she turned and made her way back down the path toward her father's property. He watched her go, loving the way her sunny yellow gown swished back and forth as she walked, giving subtle glimpses of her figure.

"Pru," he called impulsively, causing her to stop and look over her shoulder in question. "You look very well in yellow. You should wear it more often."

Her grin was as bright as the sun itself, and he reveled in the knowledge that he had elicited it.

He set his hands to his hips and exhaled as she carried on her way. Tomorrow night, she planned to dance barefoot beneath the full moon. Of course, everyone knew that a proper dance required two people. Lucky for her, he knew of a volunteer who was more than happy to join in.

\*\*\*

"What *are* you woolgathering about, Prudence?" Mama scowled at her across the pile of new fabric Mrs. Hedgepeth had brought by the house for their approval. "Can't you see we have much to do today?"

Blinking, Prudence glanced away from the wet, dreary landscape beyond the rain-streaked window and tried to piece together whatever it was her mother had been saying while Prudence had been thinking of yesterday's picnic. Something about . . . fabric, perhaps? Or flowers? The wedding breakfast menu, by chance?

Drat—it could have been anything.

Sending her mother an apologetic cringe, she said, "I'm so sorry. I was just thinking about . . . the squire's gardens. Do you think there are roses?"

It was the perfect distraction. Mama's pinched lips instantly eased as she gave the question due consideration. Anything having to do with the squire was always worthy of discussion. "Yes, I believe there are. But as mistress, you may direct the gardener to add more if you like. In fact, it will be an excellent opportunity to establish your authority within the household. Within reason, of course," she said with a confident nod.

"Of course," Prudence echoed dutifully.

"As for the topic at hand," Mama continued, "I was inquiring about whether or not the squire had indicated that you might be visiting London anytime soon."

Her betrothed's words from their short time alone together came back to her, heating her cheeks. He wanted her to visit his preferred *modiste*. It had been a singularly odd thing to speak of, and again she felt the same vague discomfort she had experienced at the time. Looking down to the square of greenish-blue silk closest to her, she ran a hand over it and nodded. "Yes, he did."

"Very good. In that case, I think you should go with the pink India muslin for a nice day dress, and the willow-green gauze with satin sprig for an evening gown." She sent Prudence a knowing smile. "I'm sure your new husband will be keen to show you off, and we want for you to put your very best foot forward during your first foray into society."

The image of Squire Jeffries parading her around

like a prize mare didn't exactly appeal to Prudence. She didn't want to be a silent decoration for his arm; she wanted to be seen for who she was.

She sat a little straighter, her fingers rumpling the corner of the silk. When had she ever wished for such a thing? For as long as she could remember, she had always wished not to be noticed at all. Wasn't that the goal of a dutiful daughter? But in that moment, with the phantom taste of illicit lemon cake still fresh on her lips, she wanted to stand tall and proud for the woman she was. The woman she had been these past few days as she pursued the items on her list.

The woman Lord Ashby had noticed.

Clearing her throat, she looked to her mother. "Actually, I think I would prefer the Eton blue silk for evening." Her confidence solidified, and she added, "And the daffodil jaconet for day. I've always felt that color complements my hair."

She willed her face not to betray her at the mention of the yellow fabric. No one need ever know that the viscount thought she looked very well in the color, or that she very much liked that he thought she looked very well in anything.

Mama reared back an inch or two, her eyes widening with surprise. Prudence could understand her disbelief, as she had never rejected her mother's suggestions before. But Prudence didn't back down. She met her mother's gaze squarely, holding her ground even as her stomach whirled with nerves.

The moment stretched in silence for several heartbeats. She could practically see Mama deciding how to respond. She wanted to disagree—that much was clear in the deepening lines at her forehead—but Prudence was on the cusp of becoming her own mistress. No one would be choosing things like the fabric of her gown for her anymore.

At least she hoped not. The squire did seem terribly keen on her trousseau, though . . .

Tilting her chin up, her mother turned to Mrs. Hedgepeth, who stood nearby with her drawings, pretending not to be eavesdropping on their every word. "I believe we shall go with both the willow-green and the Eton blue for evening, and . . ." Her eyes cut back to Prudence for a moment before giving a little nod, ". . . the daffodil-yellow for day, I think. It *does* rather complement your hair."

*Victory*!

Satisfaction swamped Prudence in a warm rush. She wanted to laugh with delight, but restrained herself to a demure smile and said, "Thank you, Mama. I think you are wise to suggest two new gowns for evening. One never knows when an invitation of importance will be issued, and I'd hate to be unprepared."

The praise smoothed her mother's forehead as she nodded in acceptance. "After decades of marriage, I've learned a thing or two about being a supportive wife. I do hope my example can help ease your transition."

A small lump formed in Prudence's throat, and she tried to swallow past it as she nodded. Her mother was so proud to see her marrying the squire. That was a good thing—a daughter fulfilling the ultimate duty to her parents. Yet no matter how much she told herself that she was doing the right thing, she couldn't get over the feeling that she didn't *want* to do it.

*Dancing barefoot in the moonlight.* She focused on that, her next item on the list, and took a few slow breaths. She would have her little rebellion, safely and quietly, where only she would know about it. The grass between her toes, the darkness enveloping her, and the simple delight of indulging in what *she* wanted to do. Even if the rain spoiled her plans tonight, she would try again tomorrow, and the next day, until she accomplished her goal.

"Thank you for helping to guide me, Mama," she said, ever the dutiful daughter. Her gaze shifted to the soft yellow fabric she had insisted on for her day gown. Dutiful, but no longer mindless. Starting now, she intended to have an opinion when it came to her own life.

Her parents and even Squire Jeffries may be none too pleased with it, but she knew without a moment's doubt that Ash would be proud of her. Somehow, that made all the difference.

# Chapter Seven

Warm, surprisingly humid air caressed Prudence's skin as she slipped out the little-used door in her father's study and onto the terrace. The rain today had nearly ruined her plans, but it had finally stopped around dinnertime, and when the clouds parted by bedtime, she had breathed a sigh of relief.

She would dance tonight, by Jove, albeit with wet feet.

Even as her heart beat wildly with the small but still real possibility of being caught, she couldn't contain her excitement for attempting something so daring. She'd never in her life snuck out of her own house. She'd never even had reason to leave her room past bedtime. This little outing was the very definition of breaking free of her parents' rules.

She grinned, savoring the feeling. She rather liked the idea of being just a little bit wicked. Of course, it helped that no one was the wiser. If she thought that she was disappointing someone, it would have leached all the fun from the night.

Her bare fingers skimmed the wet iron railing as she hurried down the stairs and into the rose garden. The scent of the summer blooms enveloped her, and she couldn't help but smile. The last time she had been in the garden, Ash had been at her side.

She pressed her lips together, allowing herself to picture him in the way she wasn't supposed to—as an attractive, virile, more-than-appealing young man. Just for a moment. It wouldn't do to allow her mind to wander too far down that path. As much as she liked him, as much as it made her stomach dance to speak with him, and made her heart pound to see him, he was just a friend.

Since each of them was betrothed to another, it was all he could ever be.

She followed the winding gravel path toward the gate to the lawn, her slippers barely making a whisper as she moved. The barefoot part of the evening would begin after she emerged onto the lawn, where the possibility of stepping on rocks or sticks declined significantly. She wanted to be free, not bruised-footed.

The white light of the moon illuminated the grounds quite handily, bright enough to cast shadows even. She would have known her way through the garden blindfolded, but there was a certain security to being able to see. After the murky water debacle, she preferred to know what was around her. Nothing was going to jump out and scare her now—

"Good evening."

Prudence gave a short shriek as her hands flew to her throat. *Mercy!* Almost at once she recognized that the soft, low voice belonged to the viscount, not that her still-racing heartbeat acknowledged it. "For heaven's sake, Ash—you scared the daylights out of me," she gasped, lightheaded from the sudden surge of fear that had careened through her.

Though she could barely see him, she knew exactly where he was: sitting on the bench beneath the old oak tree. He was just an inky spot against the shadows, little more than a figment of her imagination.

Her heart still clamored in her chest, making her feel as though she'd just run a footrace. She didn't know if she wanted to strangle him for scaring her or embrace him for not being a highwayman. Or worse: her father.

"My apologies," he said, coming to his feet. "I did try to speak softly so as not to startle you." Beneath the shadowed branches of the tree, his features were too dark to be read, but the humor in his voice was readily apparent.

"It wasn't *how* you spoke, so much as the fact that you are here at all. Thank goodness one can't die from fright. If it were possible, I'm certain I would have expired on the spot."

As he emerged from the shadows into the watery light of the moon, she could easily see the white flash of his teeth as he grinned at her. He was simply dressed in a plain dark coat and waistcoat, with pale breeches and his favorite boots. His shirt and cravat were bluish white in the moonlight, while his hair appeared almost black.

"I have faith that you are made of sterner stuff than that. After all, you did swim in a lake *I* never would have stepped foot in, sans the protection of clothing, even."

"Something I am trying very hard to forget," she said, only half teasing.

"Well then, perhaps we need to give you something new to remember." He paused at the gate and crossed his arms. "A certain moonlight dance, perchance?"

His meaning hit her all at once. He wasn't here simply to support her; he was here to *dance* with her. The familiar flutter in her middle whenever he was near multiplied, and she bit her lip against the sensation.

They'd never actually danced together before. At past events, they'd shared a few cordial words here, a polite comment there, but he hadn't been present on the rare occasions she attended the country dances, and the events at his home that she'd attended had never included the activity.

And she would have remembered. If nothing else, she would have been all thumbs in the face of his inherent grace. She swallowed now, willing her heart to calm and her legs to work properly tonight.

"I didn't mean a couples dance when I created my list," she said by way of meager protest. She simply couldn't deny that the idea of dancing with him was wholly appealing. So appealing, in fact, that she made no move to open the gate, wanting to keep the barrier between them intact.

"Then it's a good thing the list is open to improvement. Now then, as you might expect, I am well versed in all forms of dance. But given the circumstances, it's clear that only a waltz will do."

A *waltz?* Longing slipped through her like a warm breeze. Swallowing, she shook her head. "You must be joking. My mother would never let me participate in such a thing!"

He rolled his eyes, his smile never leaving his face. "How very provincial. I assure you, even the most fastidious young ladies and the most overbearing mamas approve of waltzing in London. In fact, it is quite expected. Fortunately for you, I am an accomplished waltz dancer and an excellent teacher."

It was so very tempting. She'd seen it done only once, but she'd read much about it in the society pages of the *Times*, to which her father maintained a faithful, if sadly delayed, subscription. *Lord B and Miss H shared not one, but two waltzes at Lord and Lady Granville's magnificent ball. Might there be an announcement in the near future? One imagines the books at White's are already filling with wagers relating to the possible match . . .*

"Pru?" he asked, pulling her from her thoughts.

She bit her lip. As much as she wanted to, she couldn't accept his scandalous offer. "You really ought not to have come. If we were to be caught, then—"

"Then someone else would have to have a reason for being out of doors at this time of night, and chances are it would be just as scandalous." He swung around, indicating the empty landscape around them, before turning back to face her with a grin. "Stop worrying, my friend. 'Tis merely you, me, and the nightingales."

"But—"

"And if someone did miraculously stumble upon us, at least we would be fully clothed, which is much more than I could have said two days ago."

"*Ashby*," she said sternly, scowling at him in the darkness. "You really *must* forget that you ever witnessed that particular incident. I can't have you continue to be part of my list if you insist on speaking of the items on it."

He stepped closer, reached around to the fence latch, and pulled it open. "You are absolutely right.

Now, let us get on with the dancing while the moonlight is cooperating."

He was irrepressible. And irresistible. With him standing so near, she couldn't seem to remember the reasons why she shouldn't waltz with him. "But there's no music. How are we to keep time?" It was a feeble protest, and she knew it.

He slipped one hand behind her back and gently led her beyond the path and onto the manicured grass of the lawn. "I know all the best waltz music by heart. I'll hum for us."

Turning to face her fully, he offered a very formal bow. "Miss Landon, would you do me the honor?" He held his hand, palm up, and waited for her to accept, one eyebrow lifted in challenge all the while.

*Gracious.* Between his beckoning hand and his winning little half-smile, he was hard to resist. And the way he was looking at her, as though he knew she had it in her to break even the most ingrained rules and do as she pleased, if only in the moment . . .

It made her want to prove him right.

Taking a breath, she reached out and slipped her fingers into his. His hands were bare like hers, and the feel of his skin against hers was momentarily shocking. She was immediately rewarded with a quick squeeze of her hand and the flash of his white-toothed smile. He wrapped his other hand around her back and pulled her in close. "Are you ready?" he asked, his voice ripe with promise and daring.

The heat of his fingers at her back was nothing short of intoxicating. She leaned toward him like a willow branch in the breeze as she nodded. This was to be her first waltz, and she couldn't think of a more perfect partner to share it with.

He drew a breath, lifted his arms, then abruptly paused. "Your shoes," he said, looking down into her eyes.

"My shoes?" she murmured dumbly, still reveling in the feel of his bare fingers clasping hers.

His lips quirked up with amusement. "If you wish to dance barefoot, you'd best remove them."

"Oh. Oh yes, of course," she said, quickly kicking them off. The barefoot part had temporarily been eclipsed by the waltzing part, but she still wanted to fulfill her original challenge.

The cool, damp grass tickled the bottoms of her feet. It was the oddest sensation—soft and prickly all at once. She smiled up at him, feeling both slightly ridiculous and utterly happy. "Shall we?"

Without another word, he swung them into motion, humming low and deep with a baritone she hadn't expected. She didn't recognize the tune, but she loved the way the melody swung lazily back and forth, like a boat rocking on gentle waves. Ash guided her step by step, his movements firm and capable. She'd never danced quite so intimately before, but it was something she could certainly get used to. She felt as though she could have been floating across the finest dance floor in London, a grand orchestra punctuating their every step.

It was beyond thrilling. Here she was, barefoot in the moonlight at midnight, waltzing with the most handsome, charming man in the county, with no one to tell her she couldn't. No one to override her desires, or make her feel guilty about such an indulgence.

And it *was* an indulgence. It was more delicious than lemon cake, more freeing than swimming naked, more exciting than being called by her given name.

This was what it felt like to be *free*. Uninhibited and unrestricted, like a bird sailing on the wind. She closed her eyes and smiled, soaking in this finite moment in time. She wanted to remember every step, every turn, every breath.

The wet grass made it easy to glide, and the viscount took full advantage of that fact. He moved her this way and that, his shoulders strong and straight beneath her fingers. The moon provided soft, ethereal light, bathing both the lawn and its two dancing occupants with dreamlike illumination.

She almost wished it *were* a dream. If it was, she could lean into him the way she wanted, soaking up the warmth and solid strength of him. She could wrap her arms around him, lift up on her toes, and steal the kiss she could never have in real life. A kiss that would make her heart sing and her stomach dance. One that was everything she had *hoped* her first kiss would be, instead of the cringe-inducing one she had received from the squire.

*The squire.*

Prudence stiffened in Ash's arms, then jerked away, horrified that she would be daydreaming of kissing him. More than that—she *wanted* to kiss him. She was pledged to another, for heaven's sake—as was he!

The viscount blinked in confusion as he stared back at her. "Are you well? Did you step on a rock?"

"Yes!" she said, grasping the explanation like a lifeline. But almost immediately the fib turned sour in her mouth, and she shook her head. Breaking the rules of propriety was one thing; breaking the rules of morality was quite another. "No. I'm sorry, Ash, I just can't do this."

He looked more confused than ever, his brows coming together as he regarded her with concern. "My apologies. I thought the waltz would be something you would enjoy."

"It is. But that's the problem." She shook her head a little helplessly, trying to think of a way to explain it. "There's being adventurous, and then there is simply torturing oneself with what is never to be. It's just . . . too tempting." Far, far too tempting. She couldn't believe she'd become so thoroughly swept away.

Understanding seemed to dawn then. "Ah. I see. But perhaps it's not so dire as all that. It's possible that once you are married, you'll be able to attend balls on occasion. It's perfectly acceptable—expected, in fact— for a young matron to take to the dance floor at such events."

Her shoulders wilted. He didn't understand at all. That was a blessing, really. There was nothing more mortifying than the prospect of another realizing one's attraction. Smiling stiffly, she nodded. "You're right, of course. Thank you for the dance, my lord. It was"—she paused, searching for a proper descriptive for such an all-consuming experience—"memorable."

\*\*\*

Ash was prepared to let the issue drop until she *my lord*-ed him. It was impossible to mistake the wooden way she said it. It was as though she had reverted to the way things used to be between them.

Setting his hands to his hips, he tried to meet her eyes, but her gaze remained stubbornly averted. "Pru," he said, wanting her to look at him.

"Mm-hmm?" she murmured, though she still refused to make eye contact. She fussed with her skirts as though wrinkles were her worst enemy

"Prudence," he said more sternly, this time earning her full attention. "Something is the matter. Have I done something to offend you?"

It was hard to imagine he had. The dance had been one of the finest he'd ever had, so fluid as to be almost magical. They had moved as though they had been dancing together for years, missing not a single step despite her lack of experience. In fact, up until the moment she had stopped, he would have wagered good money that she was enjoying herself immensely.

It would have been understandable if it really was simply about her fear of not being able to enjoy the dance again, but that didn't explain why she would pull away from him. They had become closer than he would have thought possible in such a short time, and the use of his honorific felt like a slap.

She shook her head, an unconvincing smile pasted across her lips. "No, of course not."

He crossed his arms. "I can't say that I believe you. You don't go from calling me Ash to addressing me as 'my lord' without a reason. Please tell me if I've upset you."

This whole evening was supposed to be about her enjoyment. He'd come because he thought he she would like the waltz. And, of course, because he'd wanted to spend more time with her. He loved being a part of her rebellion.

She looked down for a moment before meeting his eyes again. "I wasn't referring to the waltz," she said, her voice almost a whisper.

"I beg your pardon?" He wasn't quite sure what she meant.

"When I spoke of what was never to be, I wasn't referring to the dance."

Before he could figure out what it was she was saying, she hurried to her shoes, stepped into them, and offered a quick wave. "Good night, Ashby. Thank you for a lovely dance."

And just like that, she was gone. The gate squeaked as she slipped away, but that was the last he heard of her.

What the devil had just happened? One minute everything was just fine, and the next she was as skittish as a colt, escaping as though dogs were nipping at her heels.

With nothing else to do, he turned and started back to the property line, where he'd left his horse. What had that cryptic statement of hers meant? If not the dance, what had Prudence been referring to? *There's being adventurous, and then there is simply torturing oneself with what is never to be. It's just . . . too tempting.*

As her words came back to him, he slowed his steps, realization belatedly dawning. Could she possibly be referring to *them*? He and she, *together*?

He couldn't laugh off the thought. It held far too much truth. Such a thing would have seemed ridiculous only days ago, but much had changed in such a short time. They had truly enjoyed each other's company. Was it possible that she was feeling something more than friendly towards him? Surely not. Only . . . there *had* been something different between them tonight. Something intangible but real, something that had deepened the connection and enhanced the pleasure of the dance.

If she had sensed that, no wonder she had withdrawn from him. She had a duty to her betrothed, just as he did to his. Entertaining any other eventuality was impossible. Contracts had been signed. Her wedding was only weeks away, for heaven's sake.

She was right. They shouldn't be flirting with temptation. Too many people could get hurt—Prudence most of all. And if disappointment settled deep in his gut, well, that was something he wasn't quite willing to analyze.

## Chapter Eight

Prudence awoke much later than usual, regret as heavy in her chest as it had been the night before. She had done the right thing, she was certain of that, but that didn't make her feel any better. Last night had given her a glimpse into the life she had always wanted, but knew she could never have.

She wasn't the type of woman who dwelled in a dream world. The reality was, her future was decided, and nothing was going to change that. By accepting the squire's proposal—which had technically been issued to her father first—she had given her word to marry him. Just because she didn't want to become his wife didn't give her license to turn back on her word.

Yawning hugely, she pushed aside the covers and sat up, glancing to the window. It was a nice day, at least. Late morning sunlight poured through the glass, making the room so bright, it was a wonder she hadn't awoken earlier.

A knock from the corridor gave her a half-second warning before her mother breezed through the door, as impeccably dressed as if she'd been expecting the queen herself to visit. She stopped abruptly, her pale blue skirts swirling about her ankles as she gaped at Prudence.

"What on earth are you still doing in bed, you silly child? Are you unwell?"

Miserable? Yes. Unwell? Not quite. "No, I'm feeling fine this morning. I . . . had trouble getting to sleep last night is all." That was certainly true. She had gone over and over the dance and subsequent conversation with Ash, feeling the fool every single time. Why had she allowed things to progress as they had with him?

Her guilt at the way she had behaved last night was so acute, she could hardly look her mother in the eye. Her parents trusted her to behave respectably, and she'd very nearly thrown herself at another man.

"Well, now is not the time for lolling about," her mother said, marching to the bellpull and giving it a yank. "The squire is here, and wishes to take a drive with you."

Prudence's spirits fell even lower. Her betrothed was the last person she wanted to see just then. "If he had earlier indicated his desire for such an outing, I would have been ready whenever he wished."

Mama's hands found her hips as she narrowed her eyes. "If he wishes to have an outing with you on a moment's notice, then he very well has the right. As his bride, it is your responsibility to accommodate *him*."

"Yes, of course," Prudence said automatically, not wanting her mother to think she was protesting. In less than ten days, he would have complete say over her schedule—as well as nearly every other part of her life. Suppressing a sigh, she rose to her feet and began unbraiding her hair. She'd gotten away with quite enough rebellion lately. It was time to behave as the proper young lady again.

Less than a quarter hour later, Prudence was dressed, coiffed, and seated beside her betrothed in his open-topped carriage. He smiled over at her, though the narrow seating made it awkward to properly turn toward each other.

"So glad you could indulge my whim today, my sweet. Much to my surprise, I found I desired your company and didn't wish to wait longer than necessary."

Was that his way of complimenting her? She knew he was initially ambivalent toward her as a person, focusing instead on the business of the match, but it was clear he was warming to her.

Acutely aware of how uncharitable both her thoughts and actions had been toward him of late, she offered up a particularly bright smile. "Thank you for the offer. It's a good opportunity to get to know each other a little more."

In her dismay with the match, she hadn't wanted to spend more time with him than necessary, but that wasn't the way to be looking at things. She should be finding out what his interests were, what made him happy, what he disliked. As his future wife, these were things she needed to know.

He flicked the ribbons and set the carriage into motion. Her overly-large bonnet kept her face completely shaded, but the sun felt quite lovely against her arms. The brisk pace made for a nice breeze, and the steady clip of the horses' hooves was almost melodic.

"In a little more than a week," the squire said, his voice raised above the noise, "you and I won't have to worry about the inconvenience of separate abodes.

You'll be right there where I want you, when I want you. A definite benefit to marriage."

She nodded in answer. His description of marriage didn't exactly sound appealing to her. Would he look at her as another of his servants, there at his beck and call? The only thing she really knew of marriage was her parents' example. They cohabited in relative peace, but rarely sought each other out. Even so, it was a given that her mother always deferred to her father, and that he not only had the final say, but the first one as well.

"There are other benefits to marriage, you know," Jeffries continued. "Ever since our kiss, I've been thinking of them a great deal. I wonder, has your mother told you what to expect on our wedding night?"

Prudence managed to choke on thin air. Their *wedding night*? That was not something she wanted to think about, now or ever. The squire juggled the reins to one hand and patted her on the back with the other, making her discomfort even worse. Hastily swallowing in an attempt to bring herself back under control—and hopefully get him to remove his hand in the process— she shook her head. "It's not come up," she managed to get out, her cheeks so hot they felt burned.

The patting turned to rubbing, and it was all she could do not to bat his hand away. "That's good. I don't want you listening to whatever it is she has to say on the matter. All you need to know is that I will teach you exactly what it is I like, and I'm confident you'll be a good student."

If she could have leapt from the moving carriage and escaped this supremely uncomfortable conversation, she gladly would have. What on earth was she supposed to say? Yes, they were to marry, but he wasn't her husband yet and it wasn't appropriate to be discussing such things—particularly whilst in the out of doors.

He glanced over to her and smiled. "Such a sweet, biddable young thing. We'll suit quite well. In fact," he said, pulling his hand away in order to reclaim the reins, "I can prove it."

What was that supposed to mean? She pressed her lips together and glanced at him, dread roiling in her empty stomach. He glanced to her long enough to wink before slowing the horses and turning off the main road onto an ill-used lane.

"Where are we going?" She tried to sound composed, but her words held a distinct edge of worry. What was he planning? Going off alone was unseemly, even if they were betrothed. An open air ride on the main roads was one thing; disappearing into the forest down a narrow lane was something else entirely.

The carriage swung precariously as they bounced from rut to puddle, and she clung to the rail at her side. Beside her, Jeffries chuckled indulgently. "Just a little detour, my sweet."

Detour, her foot. The lane headed east off of the northbound road into town, though where it went after that, she wasn't sure. What she was sure of was that it took them farther from town, not closer.

Swallowing, she decided to try to reason with him. "After the rains, perhaps this isn't the best route. Maybe we should try this another day."

"Do not presume to second guess my driving," he said sharply. Pulling back on the reins, he waited until they came to a stop before offering her a placating smile.

"A woman shouldn't doubt a man's abilities. See? We are safe and sound, and more important, we have a moment of privacy."

She glanced around, unable to shake the unease in her belly. The trees effectively blocked them from sight from the main road, giving the illusion of isolation. "Do you know," she said, forcing a smile, "it's a little chilly out of the sunshine like this. Perhaps we could turn around and go back to the clearing?"

He ignored her completely, setting the brake and securing the reins as if she'd never spoken. When he was done, he turned fully toward her, his pale blue gaze openly traveling down her front and back up again. "Never fear. I shall keep you plenty warm."

At the very words, her blood seemed to run a little colder in her veins. What was she to do? Her parents had never prepared her for a situation such as this. Mama had personally delivered Prudence into his carriage, for heaven's sake.

Jeffries reached beneath her chin and untied the ribbons of her bonnet before tossing it aside. She felt more naked and exposed than she ever had in her life, including the day she had been caught in the lake.

"Squire Jeffries—"

He pressed a finger to her lips, shocking her into silence. The smell of leather and old tobacco made her want to turn away, but his hold was firm. "When we are alone like this, you may call me Hubert. But right now, I don't want you to talk at all."

Before she could protest—or formulate any response at all—he removed his hand and claimed her mouth in a hard kiss. He pressed his full weight against her, squashing her lips against her teeth and forcing her to pucker out of self-preservation.

This was all so very, very wrong. Everything inside of her rebelled against his touch, and against his kiss. She leaned back, but the hard seat behind her was unforgiving, leaving her with nowhere to go. Panic rose up inside her. She was trapped. Pinned like a butterfly in an entomologist's shadowbox.

On instinct alone, she began to struggle, desperate to escape his hold.

He chuckled against her lips, but didn't relent. Was he *enjoying* her discomfort? She pushed at his shoulder, but he only leaned into her more. His hands seemed to be everywhere, skimming along her arms, her hip, her side. When his left hand landed squarely over her bosom, she panicked and wrenched herself sideways, upsetting their precarious position in the high perch phaeton.

He grunted then cursed, rearing back to catch his balance. The loss of the weight of his body meant she was suddenly without the resistance, and before she could so much as squeak, she tumbled head over heels out of the carriage and landed with a teeth-jarring thump on the muddy ground beneath them.

"What the devil is wrong with you?" he growled, scowling down at her before bounding to the ground. He stalked around to her side of the carriage, his steps as aggravated as his breathing. "Are you trying to get yourself killed? You foolish, foolish girl."

Prudence lay there, stunned by both the impact and his words. Her right leg ached, her side felt thoroughly bruised, and her right wrist throbbed more and more with every beat of her heart.

"I'm sorry," she gasped, twisting around into a sitting position and cradling her injured wrist. It wasn't nearly so wounded as her heart. She had trusted this man, for heaven's sake! She had agreed to marry him, and he had just forced himself on her like a mindless beast.

He looked down on her, shaking his head. "I hadn't pegged you as the type to overreact, but clearly I was mistaken. I won't have you suffering the vapors every time we engage in such activities." Sighing as though thoroughly exasperated, he held out his hand. "Come, my sweet. Let me help you up."

The *vapors*? Was the man delusional? She hadn't suffered a fit of the vapors; she'd fought him like a cornered fox. And now, as she sat shaken and hurt in the mud, all he could do was lecture her?

As much as she wanted to slap his hand away, she didn't wish to make things any worse. Besides, with the amount of pain she was in, she needed the help. Reluctantly extending her left hand, she allowed him to help her up. Once righted, she lifted her chin, happy for once that he was the same height as her. "I'm afraid I have done something to my wrist. Would you be so kind as to return me home so I may see to it?"

In any other circumstance, she might have cried from the pain, but something told her not to show him any weakness. Not to reveal the depth of her upset and pain.

Sighing once more with annoyance, he nodded. "Fine, I suppose I must."

She was forced to accept his assistance again in

order to get back up into her seat. Her skin crawled where he cupped her elbow, and at the last second he gave her rear a sound pat.

Settling onto the seat beside her, he took up the reins as though he hadn't a care in the world. "For future reference," he said, setting the horses back into motion, "I do enjoy a bit of spunk in a woman. But there's no need to be quite so enthusiastic. Relax a bit, next time, and know that I'm in control."

He looked to her pointedly, obviously awaiting her response. Sitting up as straight as she could manage, she gave a single, dignified nod. She pulled her wrist close to her chest, wanting to protect both her limb and her heart.

It had been a mistake to agree to marry him, but what could she do now? The contract was signed. If she backed out—a prospect that was almost impossible to fathom—he would have the right to sue for her entire dowry.

Her parents would never forgive her for disobeying their edict to marry him. The scandal would never leave her. And her prospects for a future marriage and subsequent children would be destroyed.

The squire had been clever to wait until now to show his true colors. For all intents and purposes, she was as good as married to him already.

# *Chapter Nine*

The last thing Ash expected to see today was Prudence riding along with Squire Jeffries in his handsome high perch phaeton, her bonnet askew and her gown liberally coated in mud.

He pulled back on his mount's reins, watching wide-eyed as they approached. He realized at the last second that the squire had no intention of slowing down to speak with him, and he hurriedly backed his horse up a few steps to make way. In that brief moment as they rushed by him, his gaze caught with Prudence's, and the distress he saw there stole his breath.

What the devil was going on?

He wheeled around to set off after them, but thought better of it at the last moment. They were turning into her parents' drive, and whatever was going on would only be exasperated by his presence. No, it was much better to wait until Jeffries took his leave, then Ash could hopefully gain an audience with her alone in the garden.

The wait was interminable, but at long last the squire reappeared on the drive, going much faster than he should have. The precarious vehicle barely took the corner upright before he cracked his whip and sped away toward town.

Not wasting any time, Ash urged his mount toward his neighbor's house, anxious to know that Pru was all right. When he arrived in the courtyard, the door opened and the butler came out to greet him, his features drawn and serious. "Good day, my lord. I'm afraid Mr. Landon is out for the afternoon. Shall I tell him you called?"

Ash nodded, deciding not to contradict the man's assumption. "Yes, that would be appreciated. I wonder, since I am already here, are Mrs. and Miss Landon accepting callers? I did so enjoy visiting at dinner the other night."

The butler's mouth tightened, and he gave a little bow. "Allow me to inquire. If you'd follow me, my lord."

Ash dutifully trailed behind the man. When they reached the drawing room, he cooled his heels while the butler went to speak with the lady of the house. It was all Ash could do not to pace. He couldn't get the way Prudence had looked out of his mind. What had happened? Was it a fall, or something more serious that had muddied her gown and dimmed the sparkle in her eyes?

After a few minutes, the servant returned, his face a little pale. "I'm afraid the family is indisposed at the moment, my lord."

*Blast.* He really didn't want to leave, but what could he do? He had no right to insist they see him, no matter how worried he was. Having no choice but to retreat, he dipped his head in acknowledgement and headed for the door. As he collected his horse from the waiting groom, he glanced up to the second-story windows, holding out hope that he would somehow catch a glimpse of her. To his surprise, she was there, holding aside the curtain as she looked down on him.

He waited until the groom headed back to the stables, looked around to make sure he wasn't being watched, then looked back up at her. She gave a small, tight smile and lifted a hand in greeting. Looking around one more time, he pointed in the direction of the garden. She shook her head, then looked behind her as though she might not be alone.

He needed to know what was going on. None of this sat well with him at all. An idea came to him, and he held up all ten fingers for a moment, then two fingers. *Twelve o'clock.* He pointed to her, then to himself, then finally the garden.

She hesitated, gave a slight nod, then hurried away from the window. He would see her tonight. It was a long time to wait, but it was better than nothing. He'd already spent the last several hours thinking about what the devil was going on between them. He still couldn't answer the question. All he knew was that he cared about her, and he wished for her to be happy.

His happiness was important too, of course, but he had much more control over his life than she did hers. Mounting up, he turned his horse's nose toward the drive and headed home. It seemed once more he'd be seeing her by the light of the moon.

\*\*\*

"The doctor is on his way."

Prudence turned from the window and nodded. "Thank you, Mama. I know it is an inconvenience, but it really does hurt dreadfully."

82

Her mother made a noncommittal noise beneath her breath, eyeing Prudence as though trying to solve a puzzle. "Tell me again what happened this morning. I don't understand how one simply falls out of a carriage. You can be awkward and clumsy at times, but this is a feat even for you."

That had been the squire's explanation as he escorted her inside. *We had stopped to admire the wildflowers, and she leaned too far over and tumbled out.* Prudence had kept her teeth behind her tongue, knowing better than to contradict him to his face. She was still reeling from what had really happened, and she had no intention of incurring his anger.

Drawing a fortifying breath, she went to the little sitting area by the fire and settled onto the settee. "It was a rather distressing incident, I'm afraid. Mama," she said, looking to her mother imploringly, "may I speak plainly with you?"

Interest sparked in her mother's eyes. She came and took a seat opposite Prudence and nodded, folding her thin hands neatly in her lap. "Of course you may. What is it?"

"The squire. He . . ." She trailed off. Heavens, there was no easy way to say this. "He took liberties while we were stopped. It was all very distressing. I tried to fend off his advances, and that's how I tumbled from the carriage."

Two spots of color rose on her mother's otherwise pale cheeks. She pressed her eyes closed, clearly distressed. Prudence's heart rose. Having her mother in her corner meant the world to her.

"What is the matter with you, child?"

Prudence jerked upright, startled by the reprimand. "I-I beg your pardon?"

Distress pinched her mother's features as her cheeks deepened in color. She looked embarrassed and miserable and so terribly disappointed that it took Prudence's breath away.

"You will be his wife in a matter of days," she said, her voice an imploring whisper. "Of course he might expect a little more . . . *freedom* with your person. What is the matter with you, fighting him off like some sort of strong-willed child?"

Mortification swamped Prudence. The chastisement stung like a slap to her conscience. "But . . . he was so very *insistent*. He kissed me, and touched me against my wishes." The unfairness of her mother's reaction made her say more than she wanted, but she needed Mama to understand why she had felt the need to stand up for herself.

A bit of sympathy softened her mother's eyes, and she leaned forward and patted Prudence's knee. All the while, her cheeks burned a violent pink. "When it is your wedding night, you'll see that what happened today was simply part of what goes on between a man and his wife."

She cleared her throat, obviously uncomfortable, but carried on anyway. "You were unprepared, is all. Now you will know more of what to expect, and it won't seem so alarming. Just be still and allow him to carry on, and everything will be all right."

Surely she wasn't being serious. This type of behavior couldn't possibly be the norm. "But I don't like the way it made me feel. It felt *wrong*." Prudence had always done what was asked of her, but this seemed to be going too far.

"Of course it did. That is the natural reaction for a gently raised woman. The female is charged with keeping herself chaste until marriage, and it's hard to let go of that. In time, I suspect you will find a measure of enjoyment in the act." She stood up abruptly, her face still shockingly pink. "And that is all that we need say on the matter. You may stay up here and rest, and I'll show the doctor up when he arrives."

Prudence swallowed past her disappointment and nodded. The fierce throbbing of her wrist was secondary to the emotional pain right now. Was what happened this morning really so expected? Did every woman feel that way about her husband's advances?

No, she was sure that wasn't true. She had seen Ash's step-brother and his wife together. They were in love, clearly and obviously so, and they seemed to always want to be in each other's company. Perhaps if there was love or even just physical attraction, that would make things different.

She thought of Ash, and her acute desire to be kissed by him last night. If she felt that way about her future husband, she wouldn't need to be forced into anything. She exhaled and leaned against the comfortable cushions of the settee, cradling her wrist against her middle.

Mama had been so confident when she spoke of a woman's reluctance in these matters. She hadn't even been surprised by the squire's advances. Was Prudence's reaction really just a product of her unpreparedness and surprise? Had it been compounded by her unseemly attraction to Ash?

It was possible.

And in that case, perhaps she truly did have a duty to work through this. She had made a promise, and she had no real choice but to follow through on it.

After all, she was a dutiful daughter, and that was what a dutiful daughter did.

The list popped into her mind, and she almost smiled. Thank goodness for the last item. She had a feeling she would need the liquid courage that spirits offered before walking down the aisle to Squire Hubert Jeffries.

## *Chapter Ten*

Ash paced back and forth beneath the oak tree, anxious to know whether Prudence would come or not. It was already ten minutes past midnight, and there wasn't a single movement from the garden. He'd thought about her all day, wondering off and on what the devil had happened to her, and whether or not she was well. The look she had given him as they passed on the road simply would not leave his mind.

At long last, he saw a pale figure moving down the garden path. He hurried forward to meet her at the gate, but came up short when he saw the white sling holding her right arm against her front.

"Good Lord, Prudence—what happened to you?"

Her smile was dim, not nearly as welcoming as he'd become accustomed to. Was she in a terrible amount of pain?

"'Tis only a sprain, thank goodness. I fell from the squire's carriage today, I'm afraid." Though the watery light of the moon whitewashed everything, he would have sworn that her face seemed extra pale. Certainly she was subdued. He briefly considered wrapping her in a comforting embrace, but quickly dismissed the idea. He didn't want to risk hurting her any more than she already was.

"Well, based on the way the man careened out of your drive today, it's little wonder you were hurt. What happened, exactly?"

She shook her head. "I'd rather not talk about it. Suffice it to say, it was all my fault."

He made a sound of disbelief. "I don't believe that for a minute. In all my years on this planet, I've never known a person to simply tumble from a carriage without cause from the driver." At least not without the aid of drink.

"We weren't even moving at the time. I was foolish, and I'll know to be more careful next time."

Who was this stiff and stilted young woman before him? Where was the daring and sweet girl he had so come to enjoy? Something about the way she was holding herself, about the careful word choice and, more than anything, that look she had given him earlier, told him there was more to the story than she was letting on.

Allowing the subject to drop for a moment, he held out his arm. She accepted, albeit with noticeable hesitance, and allowed him to guide them beneath the tree to the wrought iron bench. He waited while she took a seat, then settled down beside her, turning his body so he could more easily see her as they conversed.

"Now, would you like to tell me what really happened?"

Her eyes widened before she quickly dropped her gaze to her lap. "It's a personal matter, really. I would rather not discuss it."

"Come now. I've seen your bare shoulders, watched as you ate an entire plate of dessert, and danced with you at midnight in this very spot. What could possibly be so personal that you don't wish to discuss it?"

He saw the tiny flare of temper in her gaze before she snuffed it out. "I am about to marry the squire, Ash. The things that go on between us are none of your business."

A hot, sharp stab of something very close to jealousy flashed through him. He didn't want to analyze it, but he did suddenly want to put his fist in Jeffries's face. If the bastard did anything to hurt her . . .

"Pru, what did he do to you? Tell me now, or I swear I will march to his house this very night and call him out."

"What?" she said, snapping to attention. "Don't you dare! Nothing out of the ordinary occurred today, I can assure you."

"Good. Then you won't mind telling me about it." He crossed his arms stubbornly, refusing to back down. Something was very wrong. He sensed it as surely as he could feel the cool night breeze against his skin. He felt fiercely protective of her just then, and was considering calling the man out even if she did tell him what happened.

She pressed her good hand to her eyes, shaking her head. "Nothing of note. We are to be married in a matter of days, so of course he should want some time alone. It is to be expected." She sounded as though she were repeating someone else's words.

His eyes narrowed. "Did he do something you were uncomfortable with?"

Her short, hollow laugh pierced his heart. "Didn't you know? As a female, it is only right and expected that I should be uncomfortable with the physical aspects of a relationship."

"What utter drivel."

She gaped at him, clearly shocked at his response. He leaned forward, wanting her to hear what he was saying. To really listen, and not retreat into this odd, introspective mood of hers.

"Whoever told you that knows nothing of matters of the heart. If a woman wants to be with a man, the thought should be very, *very* comfortable. The idea of his touch should lift her heart, the thought of his kiss should bring butterflies to her stomach. She should want to be with him above all others."

He slipped a hand beneath the fingers of her left hand and squeezed. "Whatever happened today that caused you to fall from the carriage isn't the way things have to be. You deserve more than that. You deserve to feel all those warm and good things about the man you are to marry, just as he should feel the same way about you."

He flexed his fingers, tucking her hand into his. It felt completely natural to touch her like this. To be beside her in the garden at midnight, doing nothing more than talking. Blowing out a breath, he met those beautiful eyes of hers, which were luminous even in the moonlight.

"Haven't you ever *wanted* to be with a man? Thought about him when he wasn't near, and had trouble tearing your gaze from him when he was? Haven't you ever dreamed of kissing him with such longing it was hard to breathe?"

God knew he'd enjoyed the company of women in the past, but that wasn't what inspired his questions.

Sitting here, with Prudence's hand tucked in his, he realized that he was describing the way he felt when he was with her. It was so unexpected, he didn't even know what to think about it, but he was honest enough to admit the truth of it.

God help him, but he was more than a little attracted to the girl next door.

*** 

Prudence was losing herself again.

In his eyes, in his touch, in the soft, gentle sound of his voice. This was why she almost hadn't come. This was why she knew she *shouldn't* have come. She was drawn to him in every way he had just described. It was as though he could see exactly how he affected her, and had given words to those emotions.

How had he known? Had he somehow felt them as well?

This was all so very dangerous. She should have listened to her mother and simply focused on the man she would marry, not the man she desperately wished she could be with. She swallowed, trying to draw on her dwindling ability to resist that unerring charm of his.

But he reached out, tucking an escaped lock of hair behind her ear, effectively wiping out her defenses. "Haven't you ever wanted someone so badly, you didn't *want* to leave his side?"

Her breathing quickened as she stared back at him in the darkness, lost in the feeling of his bare skin against her temple. Her lips parted, but no words came to her. She wanted to say *yes*, she had known each of the desires he had spoken of. Yes, she felt them all over the last few days. Even now she felt them as she sat utterly still, soaking in his presence as parched earth welcomed rain. After the misery of the day, the emotions assailing her now were all the more poignant.

She wanted to lean forward. She wanted to close her eyes and wait, to have him close the distance between them of his own volition because he was feeling the exact same desires, blast it. Looking in his eyes, she knew she wasn't the only one feeling something. The emotion in his darkened gaze sent a sparkling frisson of awareness straight through her.

He slid his fingers ever so slowly down the curve of her jaw. His touch was as light as air, more a suggestion than anything. When his fingers reached her chin, he paused, then gently urged her to tilt her head back. She didn't resist, didn't even breathe. How could she, when her whole body seemed to be thoroughly beneath his spell?

"Wanted him so much," he continued, his voice a mere whisper in the darkness, "that all the rules just fell away, until it was just you and him and the unspoken connection burning between you?"

She licked her lips, wanting to tell him yes, but knowing she'd never be able to come back from such a confession. "Have you?" she murmured instead.

A ghost of a smile flitted across his face. "Definitely." He drew a slow breath, then reluctantly dropped his hand. It joined his other, both of them wrapping securely around her left hand. "Which is why I can't stand to see you stuck in a situation that would deny you such a thing. Anyone as sweet and lovely as you deserves happiness."

The tenderness in his voice somehow made things

worse. Did he think she didn't *want* all those things? Every part of her was crying out for them, yet she had to face reality. She had given her word and for better or worse—much, much worse—her fate was decided.

"Since when do we get what we deserve in life? If that were the case, nothing bad would ever happen to good people, and vice versa. I am marrying the man I have chosen, and it matters not how he makes me feel."

A frown tugged at the corners of his mouth. The connection that had so thoroughly entranced her slipped away as he shook his head. "You are deluding yourself if you believe that." His voice was surprisingly sharp, his gaze unnervingly direct. "You have to be by this man's side for the rest of your life. I find it hard to believe you are willing to endure your distaste of him in order to follow through on a promise that your *parents* probably made for you."

It was uncomfortably close to the truth. She pulled her hand away and shoved it beneath her sling. She had spent the entire evening thinking the matter through. There were so many reasons she couldn't just change her mind. She wasn't some selfish child, ruled by her own whims and desires. Breaking the rules had been fun for a short while, but that wasn't who she was. She was a woman who thought of others, not just herself.

"That is unfair. I could have said no when he asked for my hand, yet I chose not to." In theory, she *could* have said no. It was never an option in her mind, but technically she could have.

"You didn't choose his hand," he countered sharply. "You chose your parents' directive. There is a difference."

She lifted her chin. "My choices and reasons are my own. If we are only going to sit here and fight about the matter, then I might as well go home now."

He gave a quiet growl of frustration. "Because that is what you do. You retreat instead of fight. Look at you. You practically maimed yourself to get away from your betrothed today, yet you still intend to marry the man. It boggles the mind."

His censure hurt more than she would admit. Why did it feel as though everyone was attacking her today? She scowled at his shadowed form. "This is my duty and I *will* follow through with it. Why must you vex me so?"

"Because you deserve so much more," he said, his voice ringing with earnestness. "I want you to see that. To acknowledge it. To *believe* it."

"So you say, yet are you not in the same situation?" Exasperation weighed on her tone as she tried to make him see how unfair he was being. "What is the difference between my marrying the squire and your marrying your Lady Tabitha?"

He scoffed at the comparison. "She's not an ancient old lecher, for one."

"No, she's not. But neither does she have a thing in common with you. She's still a child, for heaven's sake." She pointed her good hand at him, leaning into her argument. "You are following your parents' dictates, same as I am. You don't want to admit it, but you are no better than I."

"I never said that I was better—"

"Yes, you did," she exclaimed, turning to face him more fully. "Not in so many words, but you are judging me nonetheless."

Sighing, he raked a hand through his hair, thoroughly mussing it. "Because I want you to be happy."

"And what would bring me happiness? Spinsterhood? Being disowned by my parents?" She had gone through her options a dozen times in her head. Her future was decided and the sooner she accepted it, the better off she would be.

"*Love*. Love would make you happy."

She reared back, shocked at his pronouncement. *Love*? It was almost cruel for him to bring up such a thing. He was the only person she could imagine herself in love with, yet he was as unavailable to her as the man in the moon.

She shook her head, emotion clogging her throat. "You say that, but is that not what you deserve as well? And yet you bide your time for a bride to grow up, so you may enter into the exact sort of marriage as I'm about to."

Coming to her feet, she looked down at him, regret and sadness heavy in her heart. "Before you carry on any further calling my kettle black, you may well take a look at your own pot. In the meantime, I bid you good night."

Remarkably, he stayed silent as she walked away, allowing her to make her grand exit. The true irony was, she had never wanted to be called back from a retreat more in her life.

## *Chapter Eleven*

When she'd said good night to Ash a week ago, Prudence hadn't realized that she had really been telling him goodbye. When she'd learned he had departed Malcolm Manor the very next day, without a single word to her to mark their parting of ways, the sense of betrayal and abandonment was so keen as to be a physical ache. They had one disagreement, and he simply left? She had thought they were friends.

She had thought they were more than friends, in fact. Not something she would ever admit aloud, but it was the truth.

Not a day went by that she didn't think of him, or go over their last conversation again and again. Was it possible to be right and wrong at the same time? Her heart ached not to see him anymore, but what could she do? His argument had resonated with her over the past few days, but what difference did it make for them? He was still totally and completely beyond her reach.

As was her own happiness.

"Head out of the clouds, my dear. This wedding breakfast menu will not plan itself."

Prudence nodded as her mother shoved the handwritten list of meal options in front of her. Names of various meat dishes, fishes, soups, puddings, and desserts swam before her, none of them appealing in the least.

Mama pursed her lips, once again displeased with Prudence's lack of interest. "In mere days, you shall be the mistress of your own home, and choosing a menu is a very important part of that role. If you wish to please your husband, you must take care in creating the perfect menu."

It was a recurring theme over the past week. *If you wish to please your husband, you'll be diligent in choosing a proper wardrobe. If you wish to please your husband, you'll learn the names and spouses of all of his friends and acquaintances. If you wish to please your husband, you'll learn his interests and make them your own. If you wish to please your husband, you'll . . .* The list went on and on, reminding her with each new item that her only purpose in life from now on was to make her husband happy.

But the problem was, her betrothed was utterly unconcerned with what might please *her*. Unbidden, Ash's words came back to her again: *I want you to be happy*. Yes, he had argued with her. Yes, he had tempted her with things she could never have. But he was the only person in her life that had ever shown a care for her happiness.

Even she hadn't been so concerned.

But looking into the future now, filled as it was with endless tasks designed to make a man she didn't even like happy, she suddenly was concerned. Why should she go through with something that would make her so utterly miserable only to please others?

What would happen if she called off the wedding? Would the squire sue for her dowry? If so, then wouldn't they both get what they ultimately wanted? Money for him, and freedom for her? The obvious problem was being unable to marry in the future without the dowry, and facing spinsterhood, but was that really worse than marriage to Jeffries?

She shuddered. No, it was not.

The other consequence would be upsetting her parents. She'd spent a lifetime avoiding just such a fate, but would the world really end if they were upset with her? Angry, even? Was suffering their censure worse than giving herself to the squire?

Heavens, no, it most certainly was not.

She drew a sharp breath, the very thought a revelation. Her hand went to her pounding heart, excitement and fear and dread and hope all careening about inside of her. Was she really considering calling things off? Did she have it in her to do such a thing?

Only two weeks ago, the answer would have been a resounding no. But now? She felt . . . different. Ready to reach for things that had for so long seemed out of reach. Her list had helped her learn to be brave, but it was Ashby who had given her courage, who had made her imagine she might deserve more than the life she was leading. If only he could be here now to bear witness to what she was about to do.

Her life was about to change.

Closing her eyes, she drew a long, deep breath, thinking of Ash's encouraging smile, drawing strength from his confidence in her. When she exhaled, her decision was made. Opening her eyes, she lifted the sheet of paper bearing the menu choices in both hands, looked directly at her mother, and tore the sheet in half.

In the end, it hadn't been pretty. Mama had wailed, Papa had shouted and threatened, and the squire had angrily laid claim to her dowry. But remarkably, the world did not end. It was a messy, emotional business, ending a betrothal. Certainly not for the faint of heart.

But had it been worth it? *Absolutely.*

She smiled now, sitting on the black iron bench beneath the old oak tree at dusk three days later, toasting herself with a third glass of sherry at a time when she was supposed to have been preparing for what would have been her last night in her parents' home. Her mother had sequestered herself inside these last few days, declaring herself far too overwrought to leave her chambers. For that, Prudence truly was sorry, just as she hated the disappointment and anger that lingered in her father's eyes.

She'd never wanted to let them down so thoroughly, but she hoped in time they would understand why she did what she did, and accept that it had not been done simply to thwart them.

Even though it was a difficult time for them all, she knew she had done the right thing. She only wished that the viscount could know what she had done. In the midst of all the upset, she would have liked to have someone with whom to celebrate her decision. Smiling, she raised her glass toward the leafy branches and said, "To Ash."

"To *me*?"

Prudence gave a startled little gasp, nearly dropping the glass in her haste to turn around. He stood only ten or so paces behind her, looking as handsome as she could ever remember seeing him. His hair was lightly tousled, his cravat loosely tied, and his stylish dark-green jacket brought out the warm mossy tones in his eyes.

Best of all, though, was his smile. She felt as though it was reserved just for her. It was a silly thing to think, given that they were the only two people in sight, and who else would it possibly be for, but it was the thought she had nonetheless.

"Handsome Lord Ashby, whatever are you doing here?" The words tripped off her tongue with a bubbly lightness. She was so very, very happy to see him. Especially in that jacket.

He grinned even more broadly, and came to sit at her side. "You've started number four on the list without me," he said, giving the stem of the crystal glass a little tap.

"Do you think I'm foxed, my Ash? I mean, my lord?" There was indeed a rather warm haze to her thoughts, like the way candlelight looked through a frosted windowpane. It was quite, quite nice.

He chuckled, shaking his head lightly. "I think I liked your first try better. And yes, I think you are foxed. Or at the very least, a trifle disguised."

"Oh. Well, I think I am a trifle foxed, too. I didn't realize how much until you got here."

She drank in the sight of him, realizing all at once just how much she had missed his face this week. She hadn't known when she would ever see him again. It could have been years—or never—for all she knew. She wanted to reach out, to trace that strong, handsome jaw of his, to feel those perfectly formed lips beneath her fingertips. Or better yet, beneath *her* lips.

Oh! But she shouldn't be thinking like that. She may be free—thanks in large part to him—but he was not. Such a pity.

"What's a pity?"

She blinked. Had she said that out loud? "Can't really say," she said vaguely, with what she was sure was a very sophisticated shrug. "Did you hear the news?"

"That you are foxed? I'm seeing it for myself. But other than that, I only just arrived an hour ago. I changed and came here on the off chance I might see you. Imagine my surprise to hear you speak my name."

"It is a very nice name."

He laughed again, clearly enjoying himself—and her. "Why, thank you. But why did you speak it? And what is your news?"

Her heart fluttered at the prospect of telling him. No one else had been happy for her, but he would be. "You made me brave," she said. "So I called off the wedding."

His mouth quite literally dropped open. One often heard that expression, but Prudence couldn't remember ever actually seeing it happen. He did have such nice teeth, though. She had always liked them.

"You called off your wedding?" he repeated, not quite sounding as though he believed her.

She nodded twice and lifted her glass. "I did. Because you thought I deserved more. I realized I agreed."

He shook his head, looking every bit as shocked by the news as she had hoped he would be. Then, quite unexpectedly, he started to laugh. The sound was low and deep in his chest, but his amusement was unmistakable. "What a coincidence," he said, slipping the drink from her hand and setting it on the ground. He stood and held out his hand.

"What are you doing?" she asked, a little bewildered. Or was that a *trifle* bewildered? "And what is a coincidence?"

Not waiting for her, he clasped her hand in his and gently brought her to her feet. She held onto him until she found her balance . . . well, perhaps for a *trifle* bit longer than that.

"Good?" he asked, and when she nodded, he smiled. "Excellent. I thought perhaps we should add another item to your list, since I managed to miss out on getting drunk with you."

"You haven't missed out," she said, waving airily toward the half-empty sherry bottle on the ground. "Help yourself. We can share my glass."

"I think," he said, not acknowledging her kind offer to partake in her sherry, "that you need to be well and truly kissed. Preferably by someone who is in love with you, and someone whom you could maybe love in return."

Her stomach dropped clear to her toes, taking some of her fuzziness with it. "Kissed?" she squeaked, unable to believe her ears. "Love?" What, exactly, was he saying? Try as she might, she couldn't make sense of his words.

"Indeed. And I know just the man to help you cross it off your list." The warmth in his eyes as he gazed down at her was enough to take her breath away.

"But . . . but . . . you're betrothed!"

"Didn't I mention? I just returned from a nice visit with Lady Tabitha. I decided someone should probably ask her if she *wanted* to marry me. And do you know what she said?"

Prudence shook her head, all the while wondering if this was some sort of dream. But his hand felt very real in hers, and he smelled exactly as he should.

"*No*. She said no. Quite emphatically, in fact. And when I asked if she would like to dissolve the contract, she burst into tears, so relieved that she wouldn't have to marry some old man she didn't even know."

"*Old man*?" Prudence gave a horrified laugh. "Did she really call you that?"

"She did. And from her sixteen-year-old point of view, I can see how she would think that."

Taking a deep, mind-clearing breath, Prudence met his gaze. "So, are you saying you are *un*betrothed?"

His hands settled about her waist as he nodded. "If that is a word, then yes, I am saying it." He tugged her a little closer, sending a frisson of delight straight down her spine. "You say I made you brave, but it was you who made *me* brave. I never would have challenged the arrangement had I not had a reason to do so.

"You, my dear, are that reason. You're my list. You're the only one I can imagine my life with, and I was quite prepared to do whatever it took to stop the wedding and convince you to be with me instead. How very fortuitous to discover you've taken care of the first part all on your own."

The pride shining in his eyes made her feel the very best sort of giddiness. His gaze softened, and he tightened his hold on her. "And I am also saying, sweet Prudence, that I managed to fall headlong in love with you somewhere along the way. The naked swimming may have helped," he added with an incorrigible wink.

Her heart pounded madly in her chest, clearing her mind a fraction more with each beat. He was in love with her? How could she possibly be so lucky? "What a coincidence," she said, echoing his words. "Because I find myself quite ardently in love with you. And very, very much in want of that kiss."

It was an understatement. Everything inside her longed for his kiss. He was absolutely right when he had said that the right man would make her heart lift. It was beyond lifted—it was positively soaring.

His smile was slow and oh-so-satisfied as he looked down into her eyes. "Exactly the words I was hoping to hear."

He pulled her close and kissed her then, making her toes curl and her ears ring. His lips were soft and warm, seeking instead of imposing. He let her melt into him like warm candlewax. She reveled in the feel of his body pressed against her own. He was a half-foot taller than she, but they somehow seemed perfectly matched, as though they had been made precisely for one another.

When his lips parted, she readily followed suit, wanting more. So much more. She wanted kisses every morning, and sweet touches every night. She wanted to swim naked by his side, and eat cake every day, and dance barefoot beneath the moon each night. And there were other things she wanted to do with him. Things she couldn't yet name, but yearned for nonetheless.

When they broke apart long minutes later, he slid

an affectionate finger along her jaw and said, "Are you happy now?"

Nuzzling his hand, she smiled wide. "I'm happier than I've ever been in my life. Which is remarkable, because I have a feeling that it will only get better from here."

His grin was full of promise. "I, for one, shall spend the rest of my days ensuring that your prediction holds true."

She lifted a brow. "Shall we create a list? Things To Do Just Because We Want To? I think that would make me *very* happy, provided we do them together."

Laughter rang out on the evening air. "I can think of nothing I'd like more."

# *Epilogue*

*Three months later*

"I still can't believe you got your father to agree to the irrigation project. You must be even more persuasive than I realized." Prudence sent a teasing smile to her husband of one week, then yelped as he playfully splashed her.

"Oh, ye of little faith. If I could convince you to marry me, why should you be surprised that I convinced my father to agree to your father's schemes?"

They had decided on a long engagement, so that they could take time to properly get to know one another. Every day her affection for him had increased, and by the time they had finally said their vows, she'd very nearly skipped the wedding breakfast in favor of an early wedding night.

Rolling her eyes, she splashed him back. "Because I *wanted* to marry you, and your father would have rather walked across nails than agree to join forces with my father."

The week after she had ended her betrothal to the squire had been the lowest in her family's life. She had never regretted her decision, but it was tremendously difficult to see her parents so terribly distressed. When Ash's proposal had come only a week after his return, all had promptly been forgiven.

Best of all, he had insisted that the squire be given the dowry without ever turning to the courts, so no one had to sue anyone else. The earl had been absolutely furious to learn of his only son's broken engagement and subsequent betrothal to his lowly neighbor's daughter, but Ash had been unconcerned. Having already had a duke marry into the family, he felt his father had enough social connections to last a lifetime.

Ash swam closer to her and pressed a kiss to her waiting lips. "I must say, our parents are the last thing I wish to discuss right now." His hands encircled her waist beneath the water and tugged her naked body against his.

They had moved to the dower house at the northern edge of the property, and the first thing her new husband had surprised her with was a rather magnificent pool that tied into one of the hot springs. She was quite certain the pool was meant for exactly this purpose. He had chosen a spot well hidden by evergreens on all sides, the clever man.

"Oh?" she asked, lifting an eyebrow. "What, then, would you rather discuss?"

He kissed her deeply, passionately, sending butterflies fluttering through her stomach. Pulling away just far enough to speak, he said, "Absolutely nothing."

Her grin was as wide as her lips would allow. "Then by all means, dear husband, do kiss me again."

His wolfish smile sent another rush of butterflies sailing through her. "With pleasure."

## *About the Author*

Despite being an avid reader and closet writer her whole life, Erin Knightley decided to pursue a sensible career in science. It was only after earning her B.S. and working in the field for years that she realized doing the sensible thing wasn't any fun at all. Following her dreams, Erin left her practical side behind and now spends her days writing. Together with her tall, dark, and handsome husband and their three spoiled mutts, she is living her own Happily Ever After in North Carolina.

Find her at www.ErinKnightley.com, on Twitter.com/ErinKnightley, or at facebook.com/ErinKnightley

Made in the USA
Coppell, TX
30 June 2020